Tian En has created a compelling work of fiction through his relatable storytelling and comedic chronicle, bound to charm any reader of his debut novel. The Super Secret Book is a force of nature with suspense lurking on every page. From the very beginning, this story will excite your imagination and have you wondering "what's going to happen next?" It's an innovative local spin on our everyday superheroes trying to be the best version of themselves regardless of the situations they may fall into. From fighting crime to romance to mystery, this book takes readers through real life adventures.

The Super Secret characters are individuals that I could relate to, laugh and learn with. One minute I was giggling at something witty Lady Damage said and a few pages later I was trying to strategize how to beat the supervillains. Tian En crafted his narrative with sheer detail, making visualisation effortless for the reader. I am a kid at heart and this story truly brought that out of me, it's the kind of superhero novel that I enjoy reading curled up in bed.

- Tasha Arora (@tashh6)

THE SUPER SECRET BOOK

Tian En

#1

SUPER SECRET STUFF

"I *love* The Shock!"

Melanie gushed as she idly flicked through the rack of blouses. A flash of silver caught her eye, and she pounced on a hot pink top embroidered with shiny sequins, The Shock momentarily forgotten. Swooning, she held it up in front of her and struck several quick poses in the mirror.

"That's not Super Secret Stuff," I pointed out.

"I know," Melanie sighed mock-exasperatedly, replacing the blouse on its hanger. "But it's on *sale*. And since we're already here, I should treat myself to at least *something*, right?"

Before I could reply, Melanie had taken off across Diamond City's largest clothing store, Amazing Fashion, her heels clicking rapidly while I struggled to keep up. We had merely been passing by on this hot Sunday afternoon when my best friend insisted we come in "just to take a look" at the latest Super Secret merchandise Amazing Fashion had to offer. I wasn't really that much into shopping, but it was difficult to avoid it when you happened to be best friends with the biggest Super Secret fan in Diamond City. After all, what were best friends for?

"I don't see the Super Secret Stuff anywhere," I said, trying to remind her why we entered Amazing Fashion in the first place.

"Don't be so uptight, Vee! Enjoy the shopping experience!" Melanie trilled with all the good intentions of an experienced shopping guru. "You should buy something for yourself!"

Melanie was wearing her favourite combination of a white tank top and a cherry red mini skirt which complimented her figure perfectly, and she had completed the look with heels several inches tall. She was immaculately made up as usual, her long lashes framing her blue eyes which sparkled as they scanned the endless array of fashion apparel around us. She would occasionally flick her silky brown hair that flowed down the sides of her face like elegant waterfalls.

I, on the other hand, was dressed in my Sunday best, which mostly meant a clean shirt, jeans and sneakers. I wore just enough makeup to look presentable without making too bold of a statement, which Melanie was apt to do. My hair was long like hers but without the soft highlights. Maybe looking ordinary had its advantages, like being able to blend into the crowd without attracting too much attention.

Many boys have called Melanie their *dream girl*. I was known as *Melanie's friend*, but I was okay with that.

Melanie and I have known each other ever since we were kids, having attended the same kindergarten, primary school and secondary school. She had always been the girly one who loved dressing up, while I had been the one burying my nose into comic books and recreating the epic fight scenes of my favourite superheroes in my room. We got along well though, despite being so different, and it was funny how our interests gradually bled into each other's lives.

Melanie developed an interest in my superheroes when they began to cast her favourite heart throbs in live-action superhero movies, and I found Melanie's endless lectures on the latest fashion trends useful for reinventing myself once we entered secondary school. Even though I preferred doing things alone, I was glad to have Melanie's company. Beside Melanie, I didn't have many friends like most other seventeen-year-olds, but I'd gotten used to it. I've never felt comfortable in a group anyway. I only needed the one best friend.

We got distracted by a colourful display of shirts. Melanie ravaged the neat stacks of clothing, but I nipped a purple t-shirt on the top of the pile, just to get into the shopping psyche. While Melanie had a list of filters when she shopped for clothes, I zoned in on anything that happened to be my favourite colour.

"Good choice," Melanie approved, stepping back to picture me in it.

"Nah," I shook my head, putting it back.

"Whoa! There it is!" Melanie exclaimed.

She skittered towards a gigantic banner that screamed "SUPER SECRET STUFF" in an outrageously large, neon blue font. That section of the store was flooded with shirts, jackets, shoes, socks and anything else that they could slap the "Super Secret" name on. They even had specially designed notebooks in six different colours, one for each member of the Super Secret.

Diamond City is famous for three things. The sale of chewing gum is banned, each citizen's first and last name starts with the same letter, and most importantly, we have the Super Secret.

The Super Secret was a team of six teenagers in colourful costumes who had been guarding our streets for a year now, and the people of Diamond City were always excited about anything related to this crime-fighting team. These young superheroes have always made taking down bad guys look like a breeze with their combat skills and high-tech gadgets, and they were allowed by the government to do so as long as they operated alongside the law.

Needless to say, the Super Secret did not kill. They would always turn the supervillains over to the police to be judged by the law of Diamond City. Our city's criminal law was one of the strictest in the world, with the most serious crimes being punishable by caning or even death by hanging. Thankfully, none of the criminals or supervillains has committed crimes which warranted such punishments, for now, at least.

Melanie was already digging through a swamp of Super Secret T-shirts while I lingered beside her.

I saw a young couple looking at a small clutch with the words "Super Secret" sewn in gold thread on the side. The girl was pointing at it and saying something while tugging on her date's arm. I could almost imagine her whining about how it was an "exclusive, limited edition" piece to celebrate the one-year anniversary of Super Secret. The boy turned the clutch over in his hands, a hesitant look creeping across his face when he saw the price tag.

Sensing a losing battle, the girl used her secret weapon, one that I've seen Melanie used many a time before. She widened her heavily-lidded eyes, gleaming with the threat of tears, and pouted. Sure enough, the boy hastened a smile and gave an assuring nod to his lover. I rolled my eyes but sighed inwardly at the happy ending as the girl squealed with joy and threw her arms around him.

It was a lovely sight, and for a split second, I tried to imagine myself in the girl's shoes, but it was impossible. I couldn't imagine any boy offering to buy me a bubble tea, much less an expensive clutch. Besides, I was *way* too young to have a boyfriend now.

"I found it!" Melanie exclaimed. She held up a hoodie that resembled The Shock's blue and orange costume, complete with the iconic diamond symbol across its chest.

The Shock first appeared on the streets of Diamond City a little more than a year ago, fearlessly taking down criminals with his unique combat style which involved defending himself using the shiny arm bracelets around his forearms. Although he seemed to prioritise defence over offense, he knew how to throw a good punch to knock out bad guys.

He always handed the criminals over to the police with a wide smile and very quickly garnered the enthusiastic support of the people and the media, who regarded him as Diamond City's first superhero. Even President Diamond herself had expressed her admiration for The Shock, saying that Diamond City was a safer place because of him.

The strange thing was, even though he didn't wear a mask, nobody could identify who The Shock really was.

Melanie rotated the hoodie in the air, admiring it from every angle. "It's beautiful!"

I eyed it, unimpressed. "It's just a sweater."

"Hello? This is from the *official* Super Secret clothing line," Melanie emphasised. "And look! It's practically sold out. This is the only Shock hoodie left!"

I couldn't help stifling a grin as she tossed me her handbag in her excitement to try on the precious hoodie. She put it on with glee, pulling the zipper up all the way and putting the hood on so that she looked like a smaller, effeminate version of the Super Secret leader.

"How do I look?" Melanie clenched her fists in a dramatic pose. "I can be The Shock's sidekick!"

I squinted. "Yeah... not so sure about that."

"What do you think his real costume is made of?" she asked, fidgeting with the laces of the hoodie.

"I don't know."

"Maybe I'll meet him one day... that would be awesome! Do you think he'll go out with me?"

"Umm..." I wasn't a stranger to Melanie's obsessive affection for The Shock, but sometimes it still scared me. Who was I to judge her, though, when I was equally obsessed with the fictional superheroes in my comic books?

"Every superhero has a love interest, right?" she sighed dreamily. "I could be his Lois Lane!"

"Sure," I laughed and rolled my eyes.

A boy in a buttoned-down shirt hovered close by and stared at Melanie steadily. He glanced in my direction for a second, but I turned away awkwardly, trying not to make any eye contact. His gaze fell back onto my friend, but it took me a beat to realise that he was actually scrutinizing the Shock hoodie.

"Excuse me… are you buying that?" he asked, pointing to the hoodie that Melanie had on. She didn't even bat an eyelid.

"Of course I am!" she replied at once.

"I'll buy it off you right now for twice the price," the boy counteroffered, whipping out his wallet, one with the words "The Shock" on the front.

"I'm sorry," Melanie smiled prettily. "But I really want this Shock hoodie."

The boy's gaze lingered on the hoodie a little longer before he sighed and walked away, defeated.

"You're sure you want this?" I mused, feeling the material of the sleeve. "It's *so* overpriced."

"Money's not a problem. I *want* this Shock hoodie!" Melanie declared determinedly. She shimmied out of the hoodie and relieved me of her handbag. "C'mon, let's go pay for it before someone else sees-"

A sudden explosion of shattering glass interrupted Melanie's triumph. Shoppers shrieked in terror as a blurred bluish figure flew into the deep end of the store and smashed into a clothing display, close to where we were, sending debris flying in all directions. I instinctively dropped to my knees and shielded my face as dust and chipped wood rained on me.

A blaring alarm went off inside Amazing Fashion, swallowing the screams of panic as people stampeded towards the exits in a mad frenzy. As my hazy vision cleared from the falling debris, I realised in horror that Melanie was no longer next to me!

I stood up quickly to get my bearings and was knocked left and right by scampering shoppers. A girl who looked to be about my age and built but with thick glasses and a ponytail bumped into me as she whizzed by, following the people out of the chaotic store.

"Melanie!" I cried, trying to be heard over the ear piercing siren. She couldn't have gone far…

A few wise guys were grabbing clothes off the shelves before dashing out of the store, and it took all I had to swallow the rising sense of injustice at the blatant theft and focused on finding Melanie. Store assistants were hurrying people towards the exit, shouting for them to move quickly.

In the chaos, I saw a child drop his toy. He tried to retrieve it but was pulled away by his mother and was swept up by the stream of evacuating shoppers in the opposite direction.

Something in me melted at the sight of the boy's agonized expression, and I dashed into the thick of the crowd to rescue the toy, a transforming toy car with bumper stickers peeling from age. I expertly dodged the oncoming human traffic, scooped the car up to safety and managed to pass it back to him. His exhilarated smile of relief glowed with thanks as he bobbed along and disappeared into the sea of people.

I waded to where it had become less crowded and spotted Melanie in the distance, standing right next to where the figure had crash landed. Thank goodness, she didn't look like she was hurt. I hurried over to where she was, but it was only when the screeching siren came to a halt that I realised we were the only ones left in the store.

"Melanie, come on! Let's get out of here!" I called as I dashed over.

Melanie tugged my arm as I approached her and pointed at the ruined clothing display, clearly excited.

"Look!" she whispered in awe, transfixed.

Lying in a limp position on the floor was a motionless teenage boy. He was wearing a skin-tight blue and orange suit with a shiny diamond emblem across his chest, and his striking orange hair gave him the halo of an angel. Melanie's eyes were popping out of their sockets. She couldn't believe what she was seeing, and neither could I.

"Violet…" Melanie squeezed my arm. "It's The Shock!"

NEXT TIME

VIOLET AND MELANIE MEETS THE SHOCK!

"That bubble tea was *so* good… why didn't we try it before?"

"Because the queue is always super long?"

"We should check out Amazing Fashion before we go home. Do you think the new Super Secret Stuff is out yet?"

"I thought it only comes out tomorrow."

"Yeah, but sometimes they release stuff early. I heard they have a hoodie that looks like The Shock's costume."

"Who would wear that?"

"Me?"

"What if it's not out today?"

"We can still go in just to take a look…"

"It's the same thing we've seen a thousand times before."

"You never know what new stuff they have, and oh look, they're having a sale!"

"Alright, but make it quick. It's not like we're going to meet The Shock."

"I will literally *die* if I meet him. I *love* The Shock!"

#2

STUCK IN TRAFFIC

The Shock stirred slowly from his position on the ground and opened his eyes. Even though I had seen him on TV countless times before, his startling quartz blue eyes never failed to catch my attention. He'd noticed us and with a groan, the costumed superhero rose gingerly to his feet.

He was tall and muscular but not overly bulky. The large orange diamond emblem across his chest was illuminated under the bright lights of Amazing Fashion, a reminder of The Shock as a beacon of hope, protector of Diamond City and a shield for the innocent. He massaged the back of his neck and dusted off fragments of chipped wood from his side-parted orange hair, all the while surveying the damage around him.

I glimpsed the gleaming S-Braces that covered the full length of his forearms. The Shock's trademark S-Braces were famed to be indestructible and impervious to large impacts and sharp weapons, so he had never suffered such a dramatic entrance before.

"Are the two of you alright?" The Shock asked

13

concernedly, stepping towards us. Melanie opened her mouth, but for once, no words came out. I tried to act natural, but it was proving to be a challenge.

My best friend and I were just an arm's length away from Diamond City's first superhero and mighty leader of the Super Secret. I suddenly didn't know where to put my hands, and my eyes darted away from his. Before we could find our voices, a cackle echoed through the now-emptied store.

"And who are the two pretty girls?" the strange voice leered.

I turned and saw a second costumed figure standing some distance away. His ridiculously bright suit sported flamboyant yellow and red flames, and his eyes were protected by oversized goggles. We recognised him at once.

"The SuperNova!" Melanie blurted.

The SuperNova was the first infamous supervillain who went up against The Shock when he tried to rob Diamond West Bank a year ago. They had quite a tussle because of The SuperNova's *Nova Gloves*, garish red gloves which somehow increased his strength such that he could punch through walls effortlessly.

The Shock eventually outwitted the supervillain and knocked him out, allowing the police to arrest him easily and confiscate the Nova Gloves. The SuperNova was sentenced to eleven months in Diamond Prison, but it looked like he was now out and back with a vengeance.

"Didn't think I could punch *that* hard, eh?" The SuperNova chortled, his high-pitched voice grating my nerves as he addressed The Shock.

His confidence level was at a hundred percent, and it took me a few seconds to realise that he wasn't wearing any Nova Gloves...

"You can punch hard, SuperNova," The Shock said. "But you won't win this fight."

The SuperNova threw his head back to laugh. "I'm not scared of you! Today will be the day I take my revenge on The Shock!"

"You don't stand a chance," The Shock held his ground. "I already called for backup."

"Then why don't I punch you somewhere *else*?" The SuperNova taunted, cracking his knuckles menacingly.

I saw both superhero and supervillain gravitate towards each other and knew that it was going to get ugly, fast. I tugged at Melanie's arm.

"Let's get out of here now!" I hissed.

"But I want to see him fight!" Melanie shook me off, her eyes glued to The Shock.

"It's too dangerous!"

"Just for a minute!"

The Shock called to us from where he was circling The SuperNova. "Maybe next time, girls," he said, catching our eye and shooting us his winning smile. "You better get to safety! Nice skirt, by the way."

Melanie's eyes sparkled. "Thank you! My name is Melanie Mitchell, and I got this skirt from-"

The Shock didn't get to hear the rest, taking off in a flash to confront The SuperNova head-on. The SuperNova didn't shy back, charging towards The Shock with a maniacal grin. He swung his fist at The Shock, but the superhero stepped out of the way in time, avoiding the attack by mere inches. The SuperNova continued to attack, swinging wildly at The Shock, who evaded The SuperNova's punches and struck him with short, sharp jabs. I cheered inwardly when The Shock managed to kick his attacker in the stomach, knocking him backwards into a display.

Melanie had frozen, enthralled, and was watching with her mouth agape. My own heart was pounding against my chest in loud, rhythmic thumps as I decided what to do.

"Let's go!" I successfully yanked Melanie's hand, ignoring my phone, which had been vibrating furiously in my jeans pocket for the past two minutes. I knew who it was, since it was buzzing in the personalised vibration setting. The phone call and my instinct were compelling me to join the fight, to help The Shock, to do *something*. But that would mean leaving Melanie alone by herself, and how could I abandon my best friend?

"We should've taken a photo with him!" Melanie grunted as I dragged her away, surprised by how swiftly she moved in her mini skirt and high heels.

A sudden loud crash caused Melanie to jump in shock and wrench her hand away from mine. I whipped around and saw that a huge glass cabinet full of handbags had been smashed into a mess of glass and metal on the ground. The Shock appeared unharmed but was moving guardedly as The SuperNova heaved another glass cabinet above his head with one hand, laughing with frenzied glee.

I gasped. The cabinet had to be at least twice as large and heavy than he was, but he hurled it effortlessly towards The Shock like a mere football. It exploded into a plume of shards as The Shock threw himself to the side just in time to avoid it, but The SuperNova continued his crusade, picking up the next heavy shelf nearest to him.

"This way!" I urged Melanie over the sounds of more furniture being destroyed.

"They're wrecking the entire store!"

"Watch out!"

But it was too late. Melanie rammed into a fallen clothes rack and lost her balance.

"Ow!" she cried, landing painfully on her shoulder.

"Come on!" I grabbed her hand and pulled her back onto her feet. "We're almost there!"

We finally made it past the broken glass entrance of Amazing Fashion where mall security had already cordoned off the area. Paramedics were tending to different groups of people, and I heaved a sigh of relief, but Melanie looked flustered.

"My phone! I can't find my phone!" she panicked, rooting through the contents of her bag. "It must have fallen out when I-"

"Get to a safe place," I interrupted. "I'll get your phone."

"But it's too dangerous in there!"

"I'll be fine, Mels! Catch you later!"

I spun around before she could respond and vanished into the wreck of a store.

The two were still fighting when I headed back, but The SuperNova's movements were starting to get increasingly reckless. He was screaming something about taking over Diamond City and all the rest of the usual supervillain talk. The Shock dodged every one of The SuperNova's attacks, satisfying himself with a swift punch or two if he got close enough but keeping to the defensive on the whole.

It wasn't long before I spotted Melanie's phone sparkling from the debris and chucked it safely in my bag. My own phone hadn't stopped vibrating. Making sure that neither of them saw me, I found the nearest shelf that was big enough and ducked behind it.

Okay, Violet. Time to save Diamond City.

I took one last glance around me before kicking both sneakers off my feet, a motion that I had perfected from the many private rehearsals at home. My top and jeans went next. Taking a deep breath, I pulled out my superhero costume from my bag and couldn't help but feel a twinge of pride as I slithered into the purple suit emblazoned with two striking green arrows pointing up, the latex clinging to my body like a second skin. I secured the matching purple mask over my eyes, my long black hair hiding the elastic strap that held it against my face. I clipped on my personalised utility belt and thigh holster which held my own special gadget, the K-Pistol, a lightweight but sophisticated gun with my initial carved on its handle.

Perfect.

The sound of more smashed glass nearby and a sharp cry of

pain from The Shock urged me to move quickly.

I rolled up my civilian clothes into a giant sushi, shoved it inside my bag and placed it on the shelf that I had just used as a makeshift dressing room, making a mental note as to which shelf to come back to when this was over. Gripping the K-Pistol with both hands, I braced myself and stepped out from my hiding spot, aiming the weapon straight at The SuperNova.

I had expected The SuperNova to wisecrack about how two of the Super Secret wouldn't be enough to take him down, but all I saw was the supervillain lying lifelessly on the ground, pieces of broken mirror scattered around him. The Shock pulled The SuperNova's arms behind his back and locked them in a Secret-Cuff, our special brand of handcuffs that were reinforced to withstand more than ten times the strength of the average human. The Shock dusted his hands with a satisfied look on his face as I replaced my K-Pistol in its holster.

I could look straight at The Shock now, but I hoped that he wouldn't make the connection between Koolara and the girl whom he just saw a minute ago. He caught sight of me and grinned, reminding me how incredible it was that I was working alongside The Shock, the one who inspired me to become a superhero myself.

"You're late, Koolara," The Shock commented as I approached the scene.

"Sorry, stuck in traffic," I said. "Where are the others?"

"I only called you," The Shock clarified. "But you didn't pick up."

"Should've called Lady Damage instead," I said. "I think she comes to Diamond Central Street often. She smells like that perfume shop next door."

The Shock chuckled. "She's at the Secret House with the rest. They're trying out The Mystery's new M-Pills."

"Oh, those are *real*?" I shuddered. "I thought The Mystery was joking."

"The Mystery, joking? *That* would be the day…"

I couldn't help but laugh. "So why weren't *we* invited?"

"The Mystery said he only made three pills so far," The Shock explained.

"So why them?

"He said their blood was more biologically compatible," The Shock replied, kneeling down to examine the unconscious SuperNova. "Whatever *that* means."

His brow furrowed in concentration as he felt along the length of The SuperNova's arm.

"Impossible…" he murmured to himself.

"What?"

"He's not wearing his Nova Gloves or any other gadgets on his arms," The Shock shook his head incredulously. "But his strength was unbelievable. I blocked his punch with my S-Braces, but he still sent me flying across a whole *block*. Before you arrived, he was throwing entire shelves at me with one hand." He waved at the wrecked cabinets that The SuperNova had used as missiles, but a grimace of pain flashed across his face as he lowered his arm.

"You okay?" I asked concernedly.

"He scraped my arm with one of his insane throws," he winced as he touched his right bicep. "But it's nothing, I'm okay now. I just couldn't risk getting punched by him again, so I was dodging his attacks instead of blocking them. His strength threw me off, but he doesn't have much when it comes to skill. He got careless like the last time, and I just needed an opening to get close and finish him off."

I gestured to the shards littered on the ground. "And you knocked him out with a mirror?"

"Hey, a man's greatest enemy is himself, right?"

A police siren blasted from outside, followed by the screeching of tires. A squad of policemen rushed into the building and surrounded us in a circle, pointing their guns at the still-unconscious supervillain on the floor.

"Another job well done, Super Secret," the squad leader congratulated us. "Get this guy out of here ASAP," he barked at his team. "My wife will kill me if I'm late for dinner again."

"Ugh!" The SuperNova sputtered, suddenly shooting up into a sitting position. I had my K-Pistol aimed at him in a flash while all the guns around him immediately cocked. He took a quick glance around and must have figured out that he didn't stand a chance against all of us even he if did manage to break free of the Secret-Cuff. He scowled and dropped his head in surrender as the police led him out, their guns still trained on him from all directions.

"I'll be back for you again, Shock!" The SuperNova burst out as he was ushered from the building, the same manic expression on his face. "He used the Super Diamond to give me superpowers! He's giving superpowers to all of us… the Super Secret is doomed!"

The Shock and I watched in silence as the supervillain disappeared from view.

Shop assistants started streaming back into the store, shaking their heads as they saw the immense damage done to the place. The boy with the toy car held his mother's hand as he walked up to us to thank us for saving them. But it was what the boy said after that which disturbed The Shock.

"Why did The SuperNova come back?" the boy asked, eyes almost welling up in tears. "I thought you put him in prison... is he going to come back again?"

The Shock got on one knee to meet the boy's eyes, taking a deep breath.

"The SuperNova will go to prison again," he answered. "Where supervillains belong. Where they will learn their lesson and become better people."

"Okay..." the boy said uncertainly.

The Shock wanted to reassure him, but he had trouble finding the right words. A pair of security guards came to usher the boy and his mother away. There were people taking photos of us from outside the store and news cameras were rolling.

"Are you okay?" I turned to The Shock.

"Yes," he stood up. "Did The SuperNova say something about a... *Super Diamond*?"

"Yeah," I replied, pondering for a moment. "He said that someone used the Super Diamond to give him *superpowers*... but what does that mean? How is it possible to have *actual* superpowers?"

"His incredible strength wasn't normal at all," The Shock

replied, dead serious. "He could have *killed* someone if I hadn't arrived in time. If he's telling the truth, then we have to find this Super Diamond and take it out of the wrong hands, or I fear Diamond City is in grave danger."

<u>NEXT TIME</u>

THE MYSTERY AND HIS AMAZING GADGETS!

"You were *stuck* inside?"

"Yeah, the fight got too intense. I couldn't get out."

"So you actually saw The Shock fighting The SuperNova?"

"Not really. I was hiding behind one of those gigantic shelves."

"What a waste! I wish I could see him fight. There was an article in Super Addict Magazine about whether The Shock has any actual superpowers."

"They're still going with those crazy conspiracy theories? No one has seen him *fly*, Melanie."

"I *know*, but he seems to be stronger and faster than most people. What if he's secretly a vampire?"

"No one has seen him *sparkle* either."

"Ha, ha… but if he's really a vampire, he can come and bite me anytime."

"Okay, I'll remember to tell him that the next time I meet him…"

#3

NO SUCH THING

"What's the matter, Koolara?" The Shock asked.

"Huh?" I blinked. I hadn't realised that I had been daydreaming.

"Scared of swallowing pills?" he teased, but his smile disappeared when he caught my scowl. "Oh, I'm sorry. I didn't know you were really-"

"No, I'm fine," I lied. "How can a superhero be afraid of swallowing pills?"

I might be a *little* afraid of swallowing pills.

We were in the Secret House, which was really just a hidden underground space no bigger than an ordinary apartment. According to The Shock, this place had been the start of a next-generation transport system that his parents were in charge of, but the project ceased early in development when they were murdered a few years ago. The murderer was never identified or caught, and The Shock inherited all his parent's assets, including this hidden facility.

"Makes me want to have my own creepy dungeon too," Electric Boy said when The Shock first led us down here a year ago.

This place had become our headquarters and a second home of sorts, one that only the Super Secret knew of and could meet at discreetly. It had several small chambers, useful for our combat training and gadget testing. Its only entrance was obscured from plain sight, and the reinforced door could only be opened by entering a secret password.

Complicated machines riddled with wires and circuits were scattered around the room, as if this was a warehouse for rejected robot parts. The huge monitor on the wall currently displayed various blueprints and diagnostics but also doubled up as a television if we ever needed a break from our training.

I was seated at the large rectangular table of the main meeting room, where I had been eyeing the Secret Dome, a glowing blue dome the size of a basketball set in the middle of the table. This glowing dome was connected to an unseen machine under the Secret House that was constantly mining diamond crystals in the ground to generate power for this entire place.

The Shock's S-Braces were plugged into a wire coming out of the base of the Secret Dome. The piece of synthetic micro-webbed armour had been severely depleted after yesterday's fight with The SuperNova, but it would only take ten minutes with the

Secret Dome for it to be recharged to its full strength.

The Shock was seated next to me and was about to say something when the third superhero in the room spoke.

"The Shock first," The Mystery said in his deep, monotonous voice. Any emotion he might have had was hidden beneath the black mask that covered his entire head, and the only feature that made up his face was two red spaces for eyes.

The hood over his head was part of a large, flowy cape that looked like it had a life of its own. The cape could be simply seen as theatrical flair, but it was also used to conceal the many gadgets attached to The Mystery's utility belt and various parts of his costume. It still puzzles me to this day how he manages to carry all those stuff and still move around as nimbly as he did.

The Mystery swivelled his chair to face us, revealing his completely black costume, save for the red gloves and boots, and of course, the outstanding red letter "M" that marked his entire torso. I always liked how there was a tiny four-sided diamond in the middle of his iconic "M" symbol. The Mystery held up a red pill that looked like a jelly bean.

The Shock took it from him. "What does this do, again?"

"The M-Pill contains a molecular level tracking serum that latches on to your cardiovascular system and tracks your heartbeat," The Mystery explained.

"I see," The Shock mused, popping the pill into his mouth.

"The tracking serum should be flowing through your bloodstream now," The Mystery said. He turned to face me, holding up another red pill. I gulped.

"You sure you're okay, Koolara?" The Shock asked.

"Yeah," I forced a smile. "Just give me the… *M-Pill*," I imitated The Mystery's gloomy voice.

The Shock chuckled, but The Mystery wasn't amused.

I swallowed quickly, trying not to think about this foreign glob of chemicals slithering down my throat. To my surprise, it actually tasted quite sweet, like a ball of sugar.

"You're sure this thing works?" The Shock asked.

"Of course it works," The Mystery replied. "I invented it."

He took out a hand-held gadget with three giant knobs below its screen, each with a red letter "M" printed on it. Neon numbers streamed across the brightly lit display as the Mystery tapped and swiped.

"What's that?" I asked.

"Your heart rates and other diagnostics," The Mystery tapped the screen, causing the various rows of numbers to rearrange themselves. "The M-Tracker will alert the rest whenever any one of us is in extreme danger."

"Extreme Danger?" The Shock repeated. "Hopefully it wouldn't come to that."

The Mystery tapped the screen again, and each row of numbers turned into a different colour. I assumed the purple row was me.

"This city's supervillains are getting more dangerous," he said. "It is best to be prepared."

The Mystery was right. Diamond City was cursed with a "supervillain plague", as the media so dramatically called it. After the capture of The SuperNova a year ago, more criminals started to pop up with their own colourful costumes, cheesy codenames and dangerous weapons, committing one aggressive crime after another. They were regarded as "supervillains".

"The SuperNova targeted the place that was selling the Super Secret Stuff," The Mystery continued, keeping his eyes on his gadget. "Not only did he want to fight us, he also wanted to strike fear into the hearts of the people, the people who believe in the Super Secret."

"That was probably only a coincidence," The Shock said. "He probably didn't even know that Amazing Fashion was selling the Super Secret Stuff."

"He knew," The Mystery said. "He meant to punch you in there."

The Shock raised an eyebrow. "How do you know?"

"He said so himself when the police interrogated him," The Mystery said. He turned his attention back to his gadget, fingers tapping and swiping away.

The Shock crossed his arms in front of his chest. "The SuperNova said that someone used a *Super Diamond* to give him superpowers."

The Mystery froze.

"That's not possible, is it?" The Shock continued.

The Mystery's fully masked face didn't give anything away.

"Of course it is not possible," he responded. "How can a diamond give someone superpowers?"

"But he wasn't even wearing his Nova Gloves when he punched me an entire block across Diamond Central Street," The Shock pointed out. "And then he was throwing huge shelves at me single-handedly. No ordinary human has that kind of strength."

"There must be a logical explanation," The Mystery said. "I am working on it."

He put down his device and reached into a drawer, pulling out two slips of paper and handing them to me. "By the way, Koolara, Electric Boy told me to give you these."

"The tickets!" I exclaimed. "My friend would *kill* me if I didn't get the tickets I promised her."

"She likes Electric Boy?" The Shock asked wryly.

"Yeah," I replied. "But her favourite has always been *you*."

Okay, Violet. That sounded super awkward.

The Shock smiled. "I like your friend already."

A loud ringing tone blared from the old-fashioned telephone on the table. The Shock picked up the call, and after a few seconds, a worried, confused look crossed his face.

"The Triple Dangers are hitting Diamond South Bank," he turned to us. "And they're moving even faster than before."

The Triple Dangers were known for their Danger Boots, lightweight shoes infused with NASA technology which allowed them to move at twice the speed of the average human. The Shock and I defeated this trio of bank robbers several months ago and put them in prison, but just like The SuperNova, it looked like they hadn't yet learnt their lesson.

"Even faster?" I repeated.

The Shock listened to the phone again, and then said, "We're on our way."

He stood up, his silky cape cascading down from his shoulders, lending him an almost regal air. "They were moving so fast, the guards barely saw what hit them," he said, eyeing The Mystery meaningfully.

"Then what are we waiting for?" I said. "Time to save Diamond City."

SHORTLY AFTER

"Prepare to feel the fury of Red Danger!" the boy charging towards me yelled. His leather jacket was a dark shade of red to match his codename, but the rest of his clothes were standard bank robber black. His mask looked like it was made from a cheap hockey mask, and his movements were clunky and impulsive, that of street gangsters.

I fell into my combat stance and aimed my K-Pistol straight at him. The K-Pistol was loaded with fifty intricately crafted stun darts, but it would only take one to disorient its target. The serum in each dart would paralyse its target just enough to make him vulnerable for a follow up attack. The Mystery had developed other types of darts with more powerful effects, but The Shock made it a rule that our gadgets didn't cause more pain than necessary to apprehend supervillains. So far, the stun darts had served me well enough.

The time spent at the air pistol range throughout my childhood made shooting a moving target easy for me, except that this time, Red Danger was a complete blur when he hit me in the stomach. I threw a reflexive punch, but he retreated with incredible speed, avoiding my fist easily. I locked my gaze on him, trying to anticipate his next move, but I couldn't even react before he zoomed around me and kicked me in the back. The impact surged through my body as I stumbled forward.

Even though the Triple Dangers were not wearing their colour-coded Danger Boots today, Red Danger's current speed was out of this world. He was everywhere at once, and I was getting dizzy trying to track him for a good shot. I had the uneasy feeling that my usual methods wasn't going to work this time, not when I could barely keep a good lock on him.

"I always forget, is it *The* Red Danger or just Red Danger?" I mused, feigning cool as I glanced around and tried to pin the red blur dashing about me. "And I'm curious how you guys chose your colours. Purple is my favourite colour, but *Purple Danger* doesn't sound very dangerous, does it?"

"You superheroes think you're all so funny?" Red Danger smirked, his voice echoing around me. "You can no longer catch me with your little gun!"

He whizzed right next to me and threw a punch, but as soon as I felt contact, my left hand swung to where he was, narrowly catching hold of the end of his jacket. He was taken by surprise, jerking to a visible halt when he failed to break free of my grasp. I twisted my grip on the jacket until I was close enough and quickly slammed my K-Pistol into his temple. The barrel of my gun met his skull, and the impact was enough to render him unconscious.

"Okay, Red Danger is out," I announced. "*Just* Red Danger, I think."

"You're getting better and better at this, Koolara," The Shock sounded impressed.

"Nah, I'm just lucky," I beamed, pleased at his approval. Although I enjoyed the thrill of taking down supervillains, I wasn't a fan of dishing out extra pain. I prided myself in taking down supervillains quickly and neatly without much mess. Besides, supervillains were people too.

The Shock was a short distance away from me and was fully engaged in locating Blue Danger, who was zipping around him in a similar fashion. Although he seemed to have lost his target, he was perfectly calm, and I could tell that he was trying to find a pattern in Blue Danger's tracks to anticipate him. I couldn't help admiring his sharp confidence, and it was something that I always strived to emulate.

Blue Danger had begun to take up the offensive, darting around The Shock and raining punches on him. The Shock endured all the hits like a boxer in the ring. He swung his fist in a wide hook, but Blue Danger hit his arm away easily. The Shock didn't give up. He was still watching closely, unafraid of the supervillain. One hit from The Shock would do it, but what was the use if he couldn't even see Blue Danger?

The Shock shot me a look, his eyes signalling at my K-Pistol, and I understood immediately. I nodded and pointed my weapon in The Shock's direction, using every ounce of my concentration to prepare for the crucial shot. The Shock took a deliberate swing and missed, but just as Blue Danger cackled and lowered his guard to attack, I took my shot, and Blue Danger yelled as the dart sank into his shoulder.

I exhaled and smiled inwardly.

"What-" Blue Danger stuttered, feeling dazed and confused in front of The Shock. His fingers found the dart that had penetrated his jacket and yanked it out. That gave The Shock ample time to swing his mighty fist into Blue Danger's head. The poor guy didn't stand a chance, collapsing onto the floor with a thud.

"Nice work," I said, heaving a sigh of relief.

"Nah, I'm just lucky," The Shock smiled. "But there is

still-"

My eyes widened at a flash of green behind him. "Watch out!"

The Shock spun around, his cape swirling in a perfect arc around him. The third of the infamous trio, Green Danger, had a knife aimed straight for The Shock's torso. Green Danger plunged his knife at The Shock, but The Shock was faster and lifted his arms in defence, the shiny S-Braces deflecting the blade cleanly.

Green Danger was caught off guard at his botched attempt, and I fired my K-Pistol at him from where I was. He blocked the shot instinctively with an outstretched arm, but he should have known better. The dart plunged into his bare palm and took effect immediately. The third and last of the Triple Dangers was starting to feel disorientated, but the scowl on his face showed that he wasn't ready to give up yet.

The supervillain tore the dart out angrily and swung his knife again, but his movements were getting increasingly slow. The Shock stepped out of the way and knocked the weapon out of its owner's grip. Green Danger threw a desperate punch forward, which The Shock blocked easily and delivered two well-directed blows of his own. It knocked the wind out of the supervillain, almost making him fall backwards.

"W-wait, I surrender!" Green Danger suddenly cried,

throwing his hands up, his face contorted with fear. "I didn't mean to be a part of this bank job! I'd changed, I promise!"

"That's convenient," The Shock said. "Should have thought about that *before* you came here."

"Please don't put me in Diamond Prison again!" Green Danger begged, cowering before the superhero. "Anything but Diamond Prison!"

"Then answer me this, how were you moving super fast without your Danger Boots?" The Shock demanded, gesturing at the ordinary trainers on Green Danger's feet. "Where did you get your superpowers?"

"I... I can't go back to prison!" Green Danger's voice trembled, muttering to himself as if he hadn't heard The Shock. "I didn't hurt anybody!"

"Where did you get your superpowers?" The Shock repeated, moving towards Green Danger. "Do you know anything about a Super Dia-"

Green Danger cut him off with a war cry, suddenly lashing out with a second knife that was hidden in the sleeve of his jacket. However, the blade never met its mark. Before either of The Shock or I could react, a quick and sudden force had pulled Green Danger backwards, and he screamed in pain, dropping the knife.

"No!" Green Danger struggled against The Mystery's grip, but it was useless. The Mystery whipped out a Secret-Cuff and locked Green Danger's hands in its rings of justice.

"You have not answered the question," The Mystery said. "How did you get superpowers?"

"You may have won today…" Green Danger smirked. "But the Super Secret won't be so lucky next ti- aaah!"

The Shock grabbed Green Danger and wrenched him down to the ground, pressing the supervillain against the beautifully tiled floor with one knee, not giving him any room to escape.

"How?!" he growled, causing my heart to skip a beat. It was rare to see The Shock so fired up, even if he was interrogating a supervillain.

"I don't know!" Green Danger blustered. "I don't remember!"

"You're lying," The Shock tightened his hold on Green Danger. "Tell us everything now!"

The Mystery and I were positioned on opposite sides of the pin-down, ready to spring forward if Green Danger had any more surprises up his sleeves, but Green Danger had given up struggling and now lay harmlessly under The Shock.

"He gave us superpowers… using the Super Diamond,"

Green Danger said. "Please, I've said too much! He'll kill me if he knew I snitched on him!"

"That is enough, Shock," The Mystery said. "Let the police handle the questioning."

The Shock continued holding Green Danger against the floor.

"Shock," I said gently. "It's okay."

The Shock turned to me, his piercing gaze softened as it met mine. He hammered the back of Green Danger's skull with his elbow, making him the third unconscious crook in the building.

"Looks like our work here is done," I chirped.

"Koolara was a good shot," The Mystery said. "As always."

"Thanks," I smiled and slid my K-Pistol back into its holster while eyeing the three unconscious supervillains on the floor. "You heard what the green one said. They got their superpowers from the Super Diamond, just like The SuperNova."

"You believe in superpowers now, Mystery?" The Shock said.

"I believe what I saw," The Mystery replied. "But there must be a logical explanation for their enhanced abilities. There is no such thing as magical powers."

"Whatever the case, someone is giving these *enhanced abilities* to supervillains," The Shock said brusquely. "The question is, who?"

The sound of police sirens and ambulances approached in the distance, and it was only then that I noticed the casualties of the scene, crumpled behind the counters and cowering in corners.

I was shocked when I saw the wounded that were being attended to. A bank teller had blood trickling down the side of his head. A woman held her broken arm to her chest. A teenager was having a tourniquet tied around his injured leg. It was more blood and casualties than I had ever seen in a bank robbery.

I noticed that our leader was disturbed too.

"The supervillains will always come back," The Shock said, and I could tell that he was brought back to the conversation he had with the boy at Amazing Fashion yesterday. "And they're even more dangerous with their newfound powers. Look at what they've done. We need to find out who has this Super Diamond and stop him once and for all, before it's too late."

NEXT TIME

ELECTRIC BOY ENTERTAINS THE FANS!

"Do you think he heard me?"

"I think so."

"If only I had the chance to meet The Shock again... I wonder if he remembers me. I told him my name, you know."

"I'm sure he heard it."

"Do you think he has many friends in his normal life?"

"I don't know, being a superhero takes up a lot of time."

"I bet he keeps his superhero identity a secret by wearing thick glasses or something..."

"Hmm, maybe."

"But surely his friends will notice that he's always excusing himself and never coming back..."

"So, I'll see you at Gold Station tomorrow?"

"Sure, but what should I wear?"

"What you usually do. You'll look fine."

"I never have anything nice to wear when I need it the most! Oh, and please remember to bring the tickets!"

#4

SOMEBODY FAMOUS

The train doors slid open with a loud hiss, allowing the crowd of busy people to step out of the train. Melanie was already waiting for me and greeted me with an eager wave, the bouncy curls in her hair giving her the fresh, glamourous look that I could never pull off in a million years. She was wearing a short party dress and her trademark high heels for the occasion, while I was decked out in a simple pale purple blouse paired with my trusty jeans and sneakers. We gave each other a quick hug.

"Did you bring the tickets?" she asked excitedly.

"Of course," I whipped them out from my bag. "See, they're safe with me."

"Thank goodness," Melanie snatched them out of my hand to take a closer look. "Why won't you tell me how you got them?"

I forced myself to laugh, only because I haven't thought of a good enough answer to that question. How could I possibly tell Melanie that I was one of the Super Secret?

Disappearing from school whenever I wanted got me into a lot of trouble with the teachers, who assumed that I was simply being defiant. I remembered the term "rebellious phase" being thrown around frequently in the principal's office. Luckily for me, my grades were pretty good, so I never got expelled.

Since graduating from secondary school, my alibi for my frequent disappearances was a "job" at a delivery company that made deliveries on demand. I often congratulated myself for coming up with such a flawless cover, although maybe I was just lucky that Melanie never pried further.

Diamond Park was a short walk from Gold Station, and we joined the snaking queue that had formed in front of its towering metal gates. A group of armed security guards was patrolling the area, scrutinising both the people in line and curious passersby.

A hulking guard with thick eyebrows and sunglasses watched us closely when it was our turn to enter. Melanie smiled at the guard, but he showed no reaction.

"Tickets," he growled.

"Here you go!" Melanie chirped.

The guard wasn't amused as he checked our tickets.

"Is he here yet?" Melanie asked eagerly as the guard cocked his head to the side and signalled for us to proceed. "Does he come in early to rehearse? Does he come in wearing his costume, or does he-"

"Hey, move along!" someone shouted from behind us.

Melanie spun around. "What did you say? I couldn't hear you!"

"Oh, I'm sorry, I didn't know you were deaf!" an unseen voice retorted.

Melanie looked like she was about to shout something back, but I yanked her forward, hoping we weren't attracting too much attention.

"Wow, some people are really *crazy*," Melanie tutted, shaking her head.

"You're telling me," I continued, dragging her away from trouble.

Melanie gasped when she saw the massive hoard of fans already gathered in Diamond Park. There were guards stationed around the outdoor concert stage, all equipped with guns and body armour. Big speakers lined the front edge of the stage platform, and two humongous screens displayed the words "SECRET SHOW" in broad daylight.

"We have to get closer!" Melanie squeaked.

"I don't think we can," I said. "Most of these people were here since this morning."

"I wanted to do that, but I didn't have any tickets!" Melanie whipped out her phone and handed it to me. "Quick, take a photo of me!"

I took her phone and pointed it towards the incredibly tall backdrop of the stage. Standing more than two storeys high was an image of Diamond City's very own teenage superhero team, the Super Secret. All six of us were posed side by side and looking as heroic as ever.

My eyes gravitated to the two tallest superheroes on the canvas. The media had considered The Shock and The Mystery as polar opposites, often pointing out that one fought crime bare-faced for the world to see while the other covered his completely. The rest of us wore eye masks that hid our true identities from the world and also each other.

"… you taken it?" Melanie's voice disrupted my thoughts.

"Umm, yeah," I quickly snapped a photo.

"What do you think he does every day?" Melanie said, switching poses and making a "peace" sign.

"Electric Boy?" I paused to think. "I don't know, fight crime?"

"No, not Electric Boy," Melanie raised her voice as the chattering around us grew louder. "I'm talking about The Shock!"

"Probably fight crime too," I shrugged, snapping several

more shots of Melanie grinning brightly.

"The Shock and Electric Boy are both super cool," she said, blowing kisses at The Shock's picture. "But I still like The Shock the most. I read somewhere that he and Koolara are dating."

I almost dropped the phone. "D-dating?"

"That's what I read online!" Melanie said. "But of course I don't believe it. Why would The Shock like Koolara? I mean, no offence to Koolara, but she's so-"

She was interrupted by an outburst of screams. As much as I wanted her to complete that sentence, I also wanted to get this Secret Show over and done with.

"He's here!" Melanie's face lighted up. She snatched her phone out of my hands and pointed it at the stage, which was what everyone else was doing. I contemplated doing the same just to blend in, but decided that nobody was looking at me anyway.

A loud pulsing beat throbbed through the park, and the strobe lights began to flash, signalling the long-awaited entrance of the young superhero as he hopped into view, sending the crowd into a violent frenzy. People behind us started pushing forward, crushing both of us to the mob up front. They were shouting at the top of their voices, and cameras went off in blinding flashes. The girl beside me elbowed me in the ribs, and someone stepped on my foot as they strained to get a better view.

"Ow!" I grunted. Obviously, nobody cared.

"Come on, you all don't have to treat me like I'm somebody famous!" Electric Boy's voice echoed around the stage to the cheers and screams of the crowd.

Electric Boy looked to be about our age. He was lean but fairly well built, like an Olympic sprinter, and the tight-fitting fabric of his green and blue costume accentuated his toned body. His dark brown hair was tied into a short ponytail, and his black mask only covered his eyes. He paced around the stage effortlessly like a runway model, striking a pose every few steps and smiling for the cameras.

Electric Boy enjoyed being in the spotlight, making him the best candidate for our very first "Secret Show", as Electric Boy himself called it. A month ago, The Shock revealed that even though he had inherited a huge amount of money when his parents died, that wasn't going to last forever. Electric Boy suggested having a fan-meet type of event for our fans, and after a month of working out the details, the Secret Show was born.

The Shock met with the government to propose the idea and even requested for extra security during the event. To everyone's delight, they agreed and were very happy that half the profits would be donated to Diamond Police Force. The first Secret Show, which marked the anniversary of The Super Secret's first appearance, was met with massive media publicity, and tickets were sold out almost immediately.

Looking at Electric Boy on stage made me wonder if I'd be up there one day as well. Although Electric Boy was appearing by himself today, the media had not been subtle about hinting for the other superheroes to appear at future Secret Shows. Sure, I would love to be treated like a celebrity, but I could never do what Electric Boy was doing now. Put me in front of a thousand people, and I'll freeze like a statue.

"Thank you all so much for coming to the first ever Secret Show!" Electric Boy said. "Each and every one of you being here means a lot to the Super Secret and to me," he winked, sending another ripple of adoring squeals. "We've got a big show ahead of us today, but first, I would like to address a very special someone in the audience..." he stopped at the front edge of the stage and looked up. "Where is Daisy Diamond?"

"Here!" a cheerful voice blasted from the speakers. The two gigantic screens switched to a clear shot of a girl who looked slightly older than me and was extravagantly dressed to the nines. She had cute purple bangs and was wearing more jewellery than I would ever own. A spotlight found her standing in the first row of the audience where she had several guards positioned around her.

"Aha!" Electric Boy said. "Daisy Diamond, daughter of President Diamond herself! Let's give it up for Daisy, everybody!"

Daisy beamed as the audience around her clapped and hooted for her. She was the President's only child and pretty much the most famous socialite in Diamond City. She was also the Super Secret's most vocal supporter and had nothing but positive things to say about us ever since we first appeared a year ago.

"I would just like to say on behalf of my family, as well as everyone in Diamond City, that we are extremely grateful for the Super Secret," she smiled prettily, flushed at being the centre of Electric Boy's attention. "You superheroes risk your lives every day to fight supervillains and protect Diamond City, and for that, we thank you with all our hearts!"

"And we'll continue to protect this city for as long as we live!" Electric Boy declared to the swell of applause. He squinted a little before exclaiming, "That's an interesting necklace you got on!"

"Oh thanks, I made it myself," Daisy said, one hand fondling the shiny object that hung from her neck.

The cameras zoomed in on the necklace which appeared on the screens for everyone to behold. The pendant was in the shape of a heart and had the letters "L" and "D" at its centre. Its silver surface glimmered under the hot afternoon sun, inviting many catcalls from the crowd.

"I made it as a tribute to Lady Damage. I *totally* admire

her," Daisy said unabashedly. "We used to be classmates."

"You used to be what?" Electric Boy sounded genuinely surprised. "Wait a minute, how do you know who she is?"

"Oh, I recognised her voice," Daisy said. "And she's been using that dark red lipstick ever since a long time ago. We hung out a couple of times. She's a cool girl. I don't think she remembers me now, though. Don't worry, I haven't told anybody who she is."

"And you shouldn't!" Electric Boy agreed. "Not even *I* know who she is."

"Say what? The Super Secret still doesn't know each other's real identities?" Daisy's mouth fell open.

"Strangely, we don't! After a whole year, we still call one another by our superhero names, like how you all call us!"

"That's so weird. Don't you want to know who the others are?"

"What's the point? Our superhero identities are way more interesting than our real identities anyway!"

"What about The Mystery? Have any of you seen what he looks like, or does he wear that mask all the time?"

"He has that thing on *all* the time. I can't imagine wearing a mask like that the whole day though, my skin needs to breathe!"

"What if he's secretly a robot, or a cyborg or something? That's why he never takes off his mask. And maybe that's why he's able to invent so many gadgets, because he's a machine himself. Or maybe an alien…"

"Whoa, you watch *way* too many movies, Daisy! But if The Mystery really turned out to be an alien robot like in *Space Savers*, I wouldn't be surprised at all!"

The crowd laughed.

"Hey, enough about the man with no face," Electric Boy said. "Are there any questions about *me*?"

"You'll answer honestly?" Daisy challenged.

"How can I lie to a pretty girl like you?"

"Okay then… are you dating Pandora Girl?"

The crowd erupted immediately, and I felt the surging crush towards the stage as the audience leaned in to hear Electric Boy's answer.

"Whoa, where did you get *that* idea?"

My phone vibrated in a unique rhythm, and my elbow brushed against the girl beside me as I pulled it out of my jeans pocket.

"Hello?"

"A train has been hijacked," I recognised The Shock's voice. "It's stopped halfway between Gold Station and Oval Station."

"Hijacked? By who?" I kept my volume down, all the while straining to hear and be heard by The Shock in the massive crowd.

"A new supervillain. Girl in black costume. Everyone in the train has been held hostage. Go now. You and Lady Damage are the closest. She's already on her way."

I glanced at my flamboyant teammate on stage, who was still trying to placate the crowd with evasive answers about Pandora Girl. "Should I ask Electric Boy to come too?"

"No," The Shock answered as if he had already anticipated my question. "There is no time to waste."

"Alright, I'll be there right away."

"Meet Lady Damage at Gold Station and go in together. This girl could be dangerous."

"Got it."

"Bye."

"Bye," I hung up, and then tugged on Melanie's arm. "Mels, I have to go."

"What? Why?" Melanie asked, still half-distracted by Electric Boy.

"Oh, you know... my job..."

"Can't you go after this is over?"

I forced a smile and tried to look apologetic. "Sorry... I'll make it up to you soon, okay?"

Melanie sighed and gave me a quick hug goodbye. "Catch you around, Vee!" she said, squeezing my arm before I shimmied off, extricating myself from the mesh of people surrounding us.

The same hulking guard greeted me on my way out of Diamond Park.

"Not your kind of thing?" he asked when I passed him.

"I have more important things to attend to," I replied with a smile.

I transformed into Koolara at the back of a convenience store, leaving my bag hanging on the edge of a window pane. Sometimes, the best place to hide was in plain sight.

I knew that the fastest way to Gold Station was by rooftop, and as I darted from building to building above the busy streets and people of Diamond City, Melanie's words from this morning popped into my mind.

Surely his friends will notice that he's always excusing himself and never coming back...

Thank goodness my secret was safe with me.

<u>NEXT TIME</u>

LADY DAMAGE AND KOOLARA IN DEEP DANGER!

"What if we ran out of supervillains one day?"

"What do you mean?"

"The Super Secret would have no reason to appear anymore... I'll never get to see The Shock again!"

"There will always be supervillains in Diamond City. Everyone knows that."

"Why do people still want to live here even after knowing about our supervillain plague?"

"Hmm... I don't know."

"I heard that some people move here just to see Lady Damage."

"Oh, really?"

"Yeah, and that's just stupid... but Lady Damage *is* very attractive."

"Sure."

"You don't think so?"

"I don't like to judge how people look."

"Oh, please. If you saw her up close, you'll definitely think so!"

#5

BEAUTIFUL DISASTER

"Are you sure about this?"

"Relax, Koolara," Lady Damage purred. "We're only walking on top of a train track."

I wasn't afraid of heights, but my feet still wobbled a little as I moved forward step by step. The train track we were on was elevated high enough for the strong winds to slam in my face. I tried to subdue my hair, but my efforts were useless.

Lady Damage had no trouble with hers. Her fiery red hair looked fabulous as always, thrown up in the wind like in a shampoo commercial. Her dark purple costume sported a tantalising sweetheart neckline that belonged on a fashion runway. I had to admit, the finely-tailored suit was not only practical but incredibly stylish, emphasising her curves in all the right places.

The hijacked train was a short distance ahead of us. I stopped fussing about my hair and focused on the new supervillain whom we were about to face.

"Do you know how this girl hijacked the train?" I asked.

"Haven't you seen the videos online?" Lady Damage said. "She somehow tore a hole in the roof of the train and just jumped in."

"Guess I missed all that," I replied. "Wonder what she wants."

"Looking at the track record of our supervillains, I'd say she wants to defeat us and take over Diamond City. Our supervillains are not the most original."

We arrived at the stationary train, and Lady Damage leapt gracefully into the air, landing lightly on the top of the train in a single bound. It was quite a height, but she made it look way too easy. She spun around and stretched her hand towards me with a wink. I grabbed hold and hauled myself up.

We cautiously strode along the roof of the train, my heart beating faster as I anticipated danger looming ahead. It wasn't long before Lady Damage halted me and pointed in front of us. "Over there."

True enough, there was a hole in the roof of the train just big enough for a person to fit through. Lady Damage hunkered down and grazed the edge of the strange opening with her fingertips.

"Yeah, there's no mistake about it. This hole was burnt open," she said.

"*Burnt* open?" I repeated. "Wait a minute, what if this is a trap?"

"Then she's going to be *so* sorry," Lady Damage tossed her head with a wicked grin. She must have caught me gulping, because she softened.

"Relax, Koolara," she stood up, patting my shoulder. "We got this."

Lady Damage stepped forward and let herself fall through the hole. I heard the clean click of her high heeled boots meeting the ground as she landed, amazed at how they hadn't snapped by now. I sat down on the edge of the opening, allowing my legs to dangle into the empty space beneath me before sliding off the roof and into the train.

"You're even prettier in person," a cold female voice sliced through the eerie quiet of the train. "No wonder all the boys love you."

I turned and saw a strikingly thin girl dressed in a tight-fitting black suit. Her hair was cut neatly into a thick bob and an excess of eye shadow plagued the outline of her eyes.

At least fifty passengers were behind her, cowering on the floor of the next carriage and shivering in silent terror. A mother was hugging her young daughter close to her, and I could just make out that she was quietly assuring her daughter that everything was going to be alright. The Super Secret was here.

I whipped out my K-Pistol and aimed it straight at the new supervillain, giving her a quick once over and trying to identify her supervillain weapon. Except, she didn't seem armed...

"You don't have to hijack a train to flatter me, you know," Lady Damage remarked coolly, never faltering in her confident posture. "My fans have online message boards for that sort of stuff."

The girl snapped her fingers, igniting a bright ball of fire which hovered above her palm. Frightened gasps rang out from the crowd behind. It was only then that I noticed the odd smell and that the floor of the next carriage was slick with oil.

"The floor..." I murmured, tensed. Lady Damage followed my gaze and understood the danger at once.

"That's right, girls," the supervillain in black purred lazily. "Gasoline. So you better do as I say, or everyone here will burn."

My finger tightened on the trigger, but I hesitated to take the shot. I couldn't take the risk of her hurling the fire and igniting the entire car anyway.

"What do you want?" I asked, still pointing my gadget at her.

"Last month, the police put my sister in Diamond Prison,"

the supervillain continued. "She has to spend six months there just for selling a few packs of chewing gum on her blog. I know the Super Secret can do something to release her. So do it, or these people here will be burnt alive." She thrust her flaming hand towards the hostages. "You don't want to mess with Miss Summer!"

"*Miss Summer*?" Lady Damage snickered. "You couldn't come up with a better name?"

"You couldn't do better than *Lady Damage*?"

Lady Damage grinned. "Since *Lady* refers to someone sophisticated and confident, while *Damage* refers to being vulnerable and fractured... no, I couldn't do better than *Lady Damage*. *Lady Damage* is two opposite worlds put together," she struck a pose as she concluded. "I'm a beautiful disaster."

Miss Summer glared.

"Enough stalling for time," she spat.

"Stalling? If I wanted to stall, I would've asked Koolara here to explain *her* name. We'll be in this train for weeks!"

Miss Summer sneered under the thick bob. "We'll see who's laughing after I burn every-"

Her threat was interrupted by the swift crack of Lady Damage's L-Whip. She lashed at Miss Summer so quickly that the supervillain had no time to react. The whip wrapped around Miss Summer's body like a lasso, trapping her arms by her side with its automatic grip. Lady Damage yanked on the L-Whip, and Miss Summer gave a shriek before she tumbled forward and was forcefully dragged away from the hostages.

"Everybody, get to the end of the train!" I shouted, ushering them in the opposite direction of the inevitable fight. They obeyed immediately, but it was going to take some time to get such a large group of people to a safe enough distance...

Miss Summer saw that her plan had been ruined, and a shade of anger coloured her face. She squirmed on the floor and managed to grab hold of the whip with one hand. With a triumphant smirk, her hand burst into flames, spreading the fire rapidly across the whip and straight towards Lady Damage. The flames ran too close to the superhero's hand, and she let go just in time, making the whip go limp.

Freed from its death grip, Miss Summer tore the whip away and threw her hands forward, sending bright balls of flames flying at Lady Damage. The orange blasts were fast, but Lady Damage was faster, twisting in the air past the flames as Miss Summer left trails of burnt holes across the train in Lady Danger's wake.

The people had gotten far enough now, and I doubled back with my K-Pistol at the ready. Miss Summer heard me and flicked her wrists, sending the fireballs in my direction. The endless hours of physical training in the Secret House paid off as my instincts kicked in. I threw myself to the side just in time to dodge the projectiles, feeling the blazing heat as they whizzed past me and hit a row of empty seats.

"You can't beat me!" Miss Summer snarled.

Lady Damage dashed at her from behind, calculated determination reflected in her eyes. Miss Summer noticed her and cracked a smile, throwing a fresh barrage of fireballs at the oncoming superhero. Lady Damage tossed herself into a forward roll, avoiding the attack with ease. She then dived towards Miss Summer, a little gadget no bigger than a tube of lipstick clenched in her fist. She winked at me meaningfully, and I turned away in the split second she set off the L-Flash, a strong red flash of light that temporarily blinded our foe.

Miss Summer cried out instinctively, using both hands to shield herself as the blast of red light hit her dead on. I wasted no time, and the flash had barely gone off when I fired a stun dart into Miss Summer's thigh. Lady Damage pinned her by her arms as she crumpled to the floor, swiftly slapping a Secret-Cuff on her.

"No..." Miss Summer groaned, writhing from Lady Damage's hold. She tried to conjure up fireballs but failed, her hands twitching feebly in the high-tech cuffs. "I can't lose!"

"Stay down," Lady Damage said.

"Please… my sister is still so young. A criminal record could ruin her," Miss Summer pleaded.

"Your sister's punishment is fair according to her offence, and she must serve it," I responded. "Besides, she could be released from prison early if she shows good behaviour, but this isn't the way to get an early release."

"The police will be arriving any second now," Lady Damage said. "If you help us, we'll put in a good word for you and shorten *your* sentence in Diamond Prison. Trust me, most supervillains would take that deal. Just tell us who gave you your superpowers."

"It's our mum's birthday tomorrow," Miss Summer gritted her teeth. "Our dad passed away a year ago. Please, I just want my family to be together again…"

"We can't release your sister," Lady Damage stood her ground. "We're sorry, but we can't do that."

"Then *I* will," Miss Summer said.

There was a loud crack as an explosion blew the Secret-Cuff apart by its sheer heat and intensity. Bits of metal shot out in all directions, and Lady Damage spun around on one foot like a ballerina, simultaneously avoiding the deadly shrapnel and delivering a perfectly executed high kick to Miss Summer's face. The supervillain's head slammed into one of the metal poles of the train, and her body slithered to the ground, motionless.

"I think she's out," Lady Damage remarked, catching her breath.

"You alright?" I asked, standing up slowly.

"I will be in a bit," Lady Damage assured, whipping out her phone and tapping a quick "all-clear" signal to The Shock, who would receive it and dispatch the waiting authorities to help clear the scene. It was only moments before we heard the familiar wail of police cars and ambulances approaching us. Relief flooded through the hostages as they were being herded out safely, and I felt comforted that they would be okay.

"Was anyone hurt?" Lady Damaged asked.

"No, everyone got away safely," I replied assuredly. "How's your L-Whip?" I eyed the singed weapon.

"It'll be alright," Lady Damage cringed as she examined it. "Mystery can probably fix it."

"I'm not going to forget that new supervillain anytime soon," I shuddered, gesturing towards the destruction around us. "She had actual superpowers, and we could have been seriously hurt."

"Then it's a good thing I kicked her in the face first," Lady Damage answered wryly.

Lady Damage knelt down beside Miss Summer and proceeded to snip off a few strands of the supervillain's hair with a mini scissors, letting them fall into a small zipper bag.

"Mystery told me to do it," Lady Damage shrugged at my quizzical look. "Shock is waiting for us at the Secret House. Let's go."

THE SECRET HOUSE

"That girl was extremely dangerous, wasn't she?" The Shock asked gravely. We were back in the safety of the Secret House, and The Shock was still trying to wrap his head around our latest encounter with Miss Summer.

"Yeah, shooting fireballs from your hands?" I shook my head. "Shouldn't that be The SuperNova's superpower?"

He chuckled. "Miss Summer's a pretty hot name too."

"Didn't match her outfit, though," Lady Damage chimed in, gliding into the room to sit across the table, her face freshly touched up. "Black's a little dark for summer."

"You did a good job explaining your name for her," I said.

Lady Damage laughed. "I wanted her to know what my name really means. Nobody mocks my name and gets away with it."

"You two handled the situation well today," The Shock said. "Oh, Koolara, sorry to drag you away from the Secret Show. Hope your friend didn't mind."

"It's no problem," I responded. "I think she probably enjoyed it more without me around anyway."

"I heard it was quite a turnout," The Shock said.

"Looked like it."

"I've heard that people move to Diamond City just to see Electric Boy," Lady Damage chimed in.

"Oh, really?" I blinked. "That's, umm…"

"Stupid," Lady Damage injected. "Why would anyone want to come live here? We have supervillains destroying the city every day."

"I don't know. Maybe some people just want to see a good show."

"You want to see a good show, just watch a superhero *movie*. So, did anyone ask if he's dating Pandora Girl?"

"Of course, but I think he gave an ambiguous answer."

"He is."

"He is what?"

"Dating Pandora Girl. Don't you notice how they always look at each other?"

I cast my mind back and tried to think of the last time Electric Boy and Pandora Girl appeared to be "more than friends", but I drew a blank.

"I guess I'm not as observant as you," I confessed, shaking my head sheepishly.

Lady Damage gave me a quick once over. "Maybe *you* should be at the next Secret Show, Koolara. Everybody loves the pretty one."

"I'm *not* the pretty one."

"No need to be so modest. You were named *Prettiest Superhero* in this week's Super Addict Magazine."

"Probably because they couldn't decide between you and Electric Boy."

"Ha," Lady Damage snorted derisively. "What do you think, Shock? Is Koolara the prettiest?"

"Umm…" The Shock shuffled in his seat. He did that nervous tic of scratching the back of his neck whenever he was put on the spot.

"I found it," The Mystery intoned, saving The Shock from a reply. He had been peering silently into the lens of a sophisticated machine for the past twenty minutes such that I had momentarily forgotten he was even there. The blue dome at the centre of the table seemed to glow a little more intensely as he fiddled with the various knobs on the machine.

"That was fast," Lady Damage remarked.

"Human hair contains a wide spectrum of biological data," The Mystery explained, sitting up straight in his chair. A cross section of a single strand of hair appeared on the monitor with blocks of numbers and symbols running all around it. "Scientists always analyse the follicle, but the other parts of the hair are interesting as well. You just need to dig deep enough and you will find that there is so much to discover."

"Is that so?" Lady Damage twirled a lock of her own hair lazily. "Want to analyse me?"

"If I wanted to, I would have already done it," The Mystery responded.

"What did you find?" The Shock asked.

"There is definitely something unusual in Miss Summer's hair," The Mystery replied, clicking a few buttons to zoom in on the cross section. "I found a tiny trace of an unknown chemical around the edge of the hair. It is a small amount, but the M-Com can isolate its core essence and match it with all the elemental structures that it has gathered before. Maybe this will give us a clue as to where her superpowers came from."

"That totally makes sense," Lady Damage said.

"How long will it take?" The Shock asked.

"About a minute," The Mystery answered without irony. "The M-Com can only work so fast."

Using a pair of tweezers, he carefully removed the strand of hair from the machine and placed it into a pod connected to his computer. He tapped a few keys and a light shone across the hair, scanning it like a photocopy machine.

"What do you think it is?" The Shock leaned forward. "Do you really think it's related to her superpowers?"

The Mystery didn't answer immediately. Even with his face completely concealed, I could tell that he was deep in thought.

"Maybe," he finally replied. "Or it could mean nothing at all."

"The police asked Miss Summer about the Super Diamond during her interrogation," Lady Damage said as she leaned back in her armchair, toying with the L-Whip that The Mystery had already fixed for her. "She looked alarmed the second she heard those words. The Super Diamond might be real after all."

"From what we know, this Super Diamond can give people *real* superpowers which they can use to hurt innocent people," The

Shock said. "We need to take it out of the wrong hands and stop supervillains from using it."

"Okay, assuming we do get this Super Diamond," Lady Damage said. "Wouldn't you want to use it to give yourself superpowers? We can become *real* superheroes, like in comic books."

"We *are* real superheroes," The Shock said. "We don't need actual superpowers to validate that."

"They all love me!" Electric Boy's voice resounded from the entrance.

"Take a seat," Lady Damage gestured towards the empty chair beside me. "You didn't miss much, just The Mystery analysing Miss Summer's hair."

Electric Boy plopped himself next to me. "Whoa, I checked out Miss Summer's photos on my way here, and she *is* kind of hot! Why can't we have more supervillains like that?"

"We have a match," The Mystery announced as the M-Com beeped.

"What is it?" The Shock asked as we kept our eyes on the monitor, trying to make sense of the codes filling up the screen.

"Residue from Galaxy Ray."

"Galaxy Ray?" The Shock repeated. "From Doctor

Galaxy?"

"Yes."

"But Doctor Galaxy is still in Diamond Prison," I reminded. "They would have told us if he escaped."

"He did not escape," The Mystery said. "But Miss Summer could have picked up the Galaxy Ray from wherever it had been used before."

I snapped my fingers, recalling our brush with the supervillain. "Diamond City Port! That's where we fought Doctor Galaxy six months ago. He was shooting his Galaxy Ray all over the place…"

"Koolara may be on to something," The Shock mused. "Is it possible that Miss Summer has traces of Galaxy Ray on her because she was at Diamond City Port within the past six months?"

"It is possible," The Mystery agreed.

"But how can the Galaxy Ray be still there after six months?" Lady Damage crossed her arms sceptically.

"The adhesive properties of Galaxy Ray make it like an extremely stubborn stain," The Mystery said. "And the residue could easily latch onto anything or anyone in close contact."

"Hey, just believe The Mystery," Electric Boy said. "He's

never wrong."

"So what do we do now?" Lady Damage asked.

"We follow our only lead," The Shock said. "We go to Diamond City Port tomorrow. Mystery, get everyone's gadgets fully charged up and ready."

"Sorry I'm late!" Pandora Girl waltzed into the room, completing the attendance of the Super Secret. "Did I miss anything?"

Electric Boy immediately sprang up to greet her, his face beaming with delight. I couldn't help but glance at Lady Damage, who shot me an *I-told-you-so* look.

Looks like I need to be more observant.

NEXT TIME

KOOLARA PARTNERS UP WITH PANDORA GIRL!

"Amazing Fashion reopens today, and they have new Super Secret Stuff!"

"I know. You've told me a thousand times."

"Let's go this evening after I get off school!"

"I can't make it."

"What! Why?"

"I have some deliveries to make this evening…"

"Deliveries to where?"

"Umm, somewhere in the east."

"Can't you go in the morning or afternoon?"

"I don't think so, they were pretty specific about the timing they wanted the packages delivered."

"Alright… but seriously, Vee, you can't be a delivery girl for the rest of your life. You're smart and you've got good grades! Don't you want to do something else? Something more?"

"Something more?"

"Yeah, you know, like a doctor, a scientist, a lawyer…"

"Nah, not for me. I've got my own dreams."

"Like what? Oh, don't tell me… it's a *secret*."

#6

NO MORE SUPER SECRET

Diamond City Port looked like it had been pillaged by savages. The famous battle between the Super Secret and Doctor Galaxy half a year ago destroyed so much that the government had deemed it too expensive to rebuild. The port had been left to rot at the edge of Diamond City, a little blemish on the face of our sparkling home.

Diamond City's strategic location had made it a crucial player in the region's sea trade, and the enormous building that we were now about to enter used to be a storage facility. It was in here that we trapped Doctor Galaxy and finally defeated him. That fight happened half a year ago, but being back here made it feel like just yesterday.

The rest of the team should already be inside by now. The Shock had wanted Pandora Girl and me to scout around the building and try the obscure back door while the rest entered through the main entrance. On the back door was a key pad with the familiar layout of numbered buttons, just like the front door. Pandora Girl pushed on the door, but it was locked. Even though this place was supposedly abandoned, the number locks were still fully operational. Odd.

"No good. It's locked," she announced, bending down to take a closer look at the number pad.

Pandora Girl's costume was cute and edgy all at once. She was dressed in a pink spandex suit with a huge yellow star on the front, matched with a dark blue bomber jacket with the sleeves rolled up to her elbows. She wore her hair in a long magenta ponytail braid and a thick fringe with orange streaks. Tiny spikes topped her shoulder pads, and seemingly random accessories studded her jacket to complete her fun and chic look.

She was the one who suggested we create and sell our own line of products to generate more cash, and although some of us were sceptical at first, we all agreed in the end that it was a great idea. Pandora Girl worked with Lady Damage to design the clothes, bags, accessories and school supplies, all bearing our name. Not only was the Super Secret Stuff a runaway success, I was also surprised by Pandora Girl's business acumen.

"That's why we have *this*," I took out the M-Matcher that The Mystery gave us. It looked like a thick calculator with fewer buttons. I pointed it at the number pad and pushed the "START" button. The gadget whirred in my hand, and a digital loading bar appeared on the screen, slowly filling up from left to right.

"How long will that thing take?" Pandora Girl asked.

"No idea," I replied. "I've never hacked a number lock before."

"The Mystery said it's not hacking," she reminded. "It's systematic hyper-speed matching."

Systematic hyper-speed matching. The M-Matcher tries every possible combination of numbers that could be entered into the number pad at an insane speed, inevitably producing the correct one at some point. I couldn't imagine how happy a burglar would be if he ever got his hands on a gadget like this.

"Do you think it's true?" Pandora Girl asked as the little machine continued whirring furiously. "That someone has a diamond that can grant superpowers?"

"Yes, I do," I nodded. "I've seen the superpowers for myself. We have to find this Super Diamond. Supervillains with superpowers are really dangerous and must be stopped at all costs."

"Of course, that's what The Shock said."

"Yeah, that's- wait, what do you mean by that?"

Pandora Girl gave me a little knowing smile and leaned forward conspiratorially. "When were you going to tell us? How long have you and The Shock been together?"

"We're *not* together!"

"Relax, Koolara. There's nothing to be embarrassed about," she assured me airily.

"I'm *not* embarrassed."

"Good."

"We're not together."

"Everyone knows what happened in Amazing Fashion."

"Nothing happened."

"Sure, Koolara."

I was about to bring up the relationship between her and Electric Boy when the M-Matcher's screen turned bright green and the door beeped, granting us access into the facility. I pushed the door open, and we stepped in cautiously.

"My two favourite girls are here!" Electric Boy greeted us enthusiastically. He was walking towards us with a big smile on his face.

"You couldn't open the door for us from the inside?" I said.

"Hey, this is a big place!" he said. "Took me a while to even find the back door. The others are at the centre of the building. The Shock gave me the awesome job of bringing the two cute girls there."

Pandora Girl giggled.

"Let's go," I rolled my eyes, eager to re-join the others.

Electric Boy continued talking as he led us through a series of doors and walkways until we arrived at the biggest room of them all, the exact place where we took down Doctor Galaxy.

The air was eerily cold, and the lights that hung high above us were, for some strange reason, still functioning perfectly. There was a tremendous pile of broken furniture in the corner, maybe the remnants of our face-off. It reminded me of the combat room back at the Secret House where we practiced on old furniture. Other than that, the room was basically empty.

"I found Dora and Lara!" Electric Boy announced our arrival.

The Shock and Lady Damage were already here and seemed to be in the middle of a conversation. Lady Damage appeared to be keeping up with a slew of her witty commentary, but The Shock turned to us as we approached.

"Anything unusual out there?" he asked.

"Other than the same number lock on the back door, nothing much," I shrugged.

"Why would the number locks still be working in this abandoned building?" Pandora Girl asked.

"Somebody does not want people entering this building,"

The Mystery entered the room to join us. "And he is not taking any chances. We are not supposed to be here."

"Don't make everything sound so scary," Lady Damage chided. "You're going to scare the kids."

"I have walked the entire building," The Mystery continued. He was holding a gadget resembling a barcode scanner with antennas. "Our theory is correct. A very small trace of Galaxy Ray is still lingering throughout this building, and it appears to be the strongest where Doctor Galaxy was defeated and his Galaxy Cannons cracked open, which is where we are standing right now. Diamond Prison gave me hair samples of The SuperNova and the Triple Dangers, and they all had Galaxy Ray on them. That means they have been here too."

"Is it safe for us to be in here?" The Shock asked.

"Yes," The Mystery answered squarely. "Galaxy Ray is just a chemically enhanced substance that Doctor Galaxy used to trap people. Its residue has no harmful effect on us. We can-"

A sound made him pause, and he cocked his head to the side, listening intently. "We have company."

"Should have called to let me know you were coming," a new voice rang out.

A figure with a white cowl that covered the top half of his

head appeared at the door. His masked face had black triangles for eyes, and his hands were tucked into the pockets of an oversized jacket resembling a creepy surgical suit. His feet didn't seem to lift when he walked, creating the illusion that he was floating towards us.

"Sorry to come in uninvited," The Shock said, immediately stepping in front of us protectively. "But this is important."

The teenager in white chuckled and stopped a short distance away from us.

"I'm Mr Magic," he introduced himself. His voice made my skin crawl. "How may I be of service?"

"We want answers," The Shock said. "Someone gave superpowers to The SuperNova, the Triple Dangers and Miss Summer. They've all got traces of Galaxy Ray on them, which means they have been to this building before, to *your* hideout. Whoever gave them superpowers made them put a tight lid on it, but maybe you can shed some light on the subject."

Mr Magic grinned. "Even if I knew, why would I tell you?"

"Because our evidence makes you a prime suspect," The Shock said. "We could bring you in right now, and believe me, The Mystery has the means to tell if you're lying. You could be in Diamond Prison for a *very* long time. We can still do this the easy way if you cooperate and tell us where the superpowers come from."

"Cooperate?" Mr Magic let out a sinister laugh. "I'm going to *kill* the Super Secret. With you lot out of my way, I'll finally be able to take over Diamond City!"

"Yeah, but there's six of us and only one of you," Electric Boy retorted. "You don't stand a chance!"

"Oh, but I do," Mr Magic smirked. He waved both hands in front of him like a magician, but instead of a dove, he conjured up a luminous block of translucent crystal between his palms, which hovered in mid-air. The shiny crystal seemed to be alive, morphing into different shapes as if it were a liquid before finally settling into the form of a long, sharp spear. Mr Magic splayed his fingers, aiming the spear at us without touching it. It looked as if he could launch it at us if he wanted to. I clenched my fists tightly by my sides and held my breath.

"Shoot that thing at me, and my five friends will take you down," The Shock said. "Did you really think you could defeat the Super Secret so easily?"

Mr Magic cocked his head, his unnerving smile revealing that he was not the least bit intimidated.

"We know about the Super Diamond," The Shock said. "We know that it gives people superpowers."

"Ha," Mr Magic chuckled as he lowered his hands, but the spear made of crystal remained suspended in the air, its pointed end still aimed at us. "So you guys are not as clueless as I thought... but do you expect me to just *give* you the Super Diamond?"

"So you *do* have it," The Shock responded. "Where did you get it?"

"He gave it to me."

"Who? Who gave it to you?"

"I'll never tell you."

"Give us the Super Diamond."

"I'd rather not," Mr Magic leered. The crystal spear flew so fast that I could barely see it moving through the air. It went for The Shock's chest but shattered into a million pieces when it hit The Shock's S-Braces instead. The Shock lowered his arms, unfazed by the attack.

Mr Magic wasn't discouraged. He rubbed his hands together, the crystal forming more quickly this time. He transformed the translucent material into two long knives which he gripped with both hands, ready to hack and slash his way to victory.

The supervillain advanced towards us with more shiny

crystal forming around his torso in segregated plates, weaving into a kind of armour. I pulled out my K-Pistol and quickly pulled the trigger. It was an easy shot at this distance, but in a split second, he had summoned a large, circular crystal shield that floated in front of him, deflecting the dart easily.

"We need to surround him," The Shock instructed. "Let's see how powerful this guy really is…"

Lady Damage dashed forward and flung her L-Whip at the crystal shield, getting a good hold on it. She jerked at it but it remained immovable. Electric Boy and Pandora Girl moved swiftly to position themselves around him. I tried to get closer, but The Shock came in front of me first, taking up the most defensive position for me if Mr Magic turned my way, as if he was *my* shield.

"Stay back and wait," he murmured. "If things get out of hand, use the power darts."

I hesitated but nodded, loading the power darts into the K-Pistol and cocking it. While my usual stun darts only disorientated the target, these power darts would send a serum into the victim's body and cause painful contractions in all four limbs, like getting huge cramps in your arms and legs all at the same time. We never wanted to cause more pain than necessary to apprehend supervillains, but it looked like the situation had finally warranted the use of a more dramatic weapon. I felt the quiet hum from my K-Pistol and steadied my grip.

Electric Boy made his move first. He ran up to Mr Magic from the back, throwing an E-Bomb near the supervillain's feet, a classic opening move whereby the mini bomb would release a thick black smoke to obscure our opponent's vision and disorientate his senses while we launched a counterattack. The stun smoke's bio-homing technology also enabled it to detect and travel towards the nearest human, so running away wasn't going to help. To protect us from it, The Mystery had laced our costumes with a chemical that repelled the stun smoke.

We didn't get to witness the sensational E-Bomb in action today, however, because Mr Magic waved his fingers at the ground, calling a block of crystal to materialise around the bomb, completely covering it up and containing the explosion of black smoke.

The crystal disintegrated quickly, and a gleeful Mr Magic took up on the offensive with a pair of crystal knives. He tossed them lightly in the air, and they spun a few times before coming to a stop in mid-air with their points aimed straight at Electric Boy.

"Oh boy," Electric Boy muttered.

The first crystal knife plunged towards Electric Boy, and he performed an impressive flying kick which shattered it. He whipped around for the second crystal knife, but it was smashed to bits by a yellow blur that soared through the air. The pointed P-Star circled back to its owner, Pandora Girl, who caught it expertly between her fingers with a smile.

"You're not the only one with dangerous flying objects," Electric Boy whooped at Mr Magic. "Show him, Dora!"

Pandora Girl flung her P-Star again, and the special throwing star that would always return to her glove sliced through the air towards Mr Magic. With a flick of his wrist, Mr Magic conjured a stream of crystal which deflected the P-Star easily. Before the P-Star could return to Pandora Girl, Mr Magic directed the crystal towards her, which rapidly solidified around the petite girl.

"Dora!" Electric Boy tried to ply the crystal away, but the growing glob of crystal swallowed him as well, trapping them both.

"Whoa!" Pandora Girl yelped as they fell backwards from the sheer weight of the crystal, unable to break out of the trap they were now stuck in.

I circled around the scene, trying to find a good shot. I wanted to get close and join in the fight, but The Shock gestured for me to stay back. Perhaps he still wanted to take down Mr Magic without using the power darts.

Lady Damage leapt forward and gave Mr Magic a flying kick from behind, but the crystal armour around his torso absorbed the impact of Lady Damage's high heel boot. A crystal sword formed in Mr Magic's grasp and he swung it at her, missing her by mere inches. The Shock also got in on the action, attacking with a barrage of punches alongside Lady Damage. The dual strategy worked. Lady Damage managed to sweep Mr Magic off his feet and caused him to crash face first into the floor. The Shock tried to pin him down, but a block of Mr Magic's crystal exploded between them, forcefully pushing The Shock away.

Mr Magic bounced back onto his feet with a sadistic smile on his face, brandishing his crystal sword. It was short-lived, however. With a crack of her L-Whip, Lady Damage made quick work of it, flinging the sword far away from him. Refusing to be beaten, Mr Magic sent a swarm of pointed crystal shards flying towards her. She gasped and instinctively dropped into a roll to dodge them, but a few hit her and knocked her off balance. Before we knew it, she too was caught in a thick stream of crystal and was rendered immobile.

With Lady Damage out of his way, Mr Magic turned his attention to The Shock and fired a wave of crystal shards at him, but The Shock blocked all of it with his S-Braces. One shard caught him in the leg, making him flinch. Mr Magic noticed it and pounced at the chance. He took a running leap, a newly formed crystal dagger in his hands, and aimed for The Shock, but The Shock twisted out of the way at the last moment and swung to slam Mr Magic down from the back, flattening the supervillain to the ground.

"Now!" The Shock commanded, but before I could shoot, Mr Magic slammed both fists on the ground, and what looked like a translucent igloo began to grow around him as a shield, protecting him in all directions.

I took my shot from where I was, and I held my breath as the power dart whizzed towards Mr Magic, but it was already too late. The crystal igloo was complete, and my power dart bounced off the structure onto the ground.

Just when I thought all was lost, a sharp cry of pain rang out from inside the crystal igloo, and Mr Magic unexpectedly crashed out of his own safe house, leaving a big hole in the wall. The Mystery jumped out of the hole and landed on Mr Magic, giving him a series of quick blows to the face. He pulled a weakened Mr Magic up into a kneeling position, and I fired a power dart into the supervillain's shoulder. Mr Magic screamed as the power dart came into effect.

"Tell us where the Super Diamond is," The Mystery demanded. "And I will stop the pain."

The crystal traps holding on to Electric Boy, Pandora Girl and Lady Damage disintegrated quickly, and they gathered around the screaming supervillain. Despite the excruciating cramps, Mr Magic managed to rummage the pockets of his large jacket, desperately searching for something. An object wrapped in black cloth fell to the ground. It was no bigger than an apple but seemed much heavier. Could it be the Super Diamond?

The Mystery pulled out the power dart from Mr Magic's shoulder and pressed a syringe against the same spot, injecting a blue liquid into him. Mr Magic immediately relaxed, his eyelids gradually closing as if he was going to sleep. He slunk limply to the ground, unconscious. I too was just beginning to relax when a sudden rumbling noise startled us.

"What's that?" Pandora Girl asked.

Before anyone could answer, the four walls around us were set ablaze, and it took me a few seconds to realise that it wasn't my imagination. The flames were real, and they were spreading fast. The room was quickly heating up like a giant microwave, and the floor beneath my boots was getting hotter and hotter. The door burst into flames and became a crackling wall of fire.

The Mystery swiftly picked up the wrapped object from Mr Magic and slipped it into one of the pouches on his utility belt. He then held up Mr Magic's left fist, which had been hidden in his pocket. Mr Magic was holding on to a cylindrical device topped with a small, red button.

"Mr Magic seemed to have activated some kind of self-destruct protocol just before he passed out," The Mystery said matter-of-factly.

"Aah! Now what?" Electric Boy wailed, skittering back

and forth in distress. Pandora Girl swept her thick fringe back, wiping off the sweat from her forehead and neck. I did the same, fighting the temptation to yank my mask off.

"Everyone stay calm," The Shock instructed. "Mystery, what's our best way out of here?"

"I have an idea," The Mystery said. "Close in, everybody."

We gathered around our gadget expert, who took out something like an oversized salt shaker with buttons and switches along its metal body. The Mystery tugged at it, making it extend to double its length, one end sporting a mini harpoon.

"Never leave home without it," Lady Damage remarked.

The Mystery looked up, trying to gauge the distance to the ceiling. We followed his gaze. The ceiling had to be at least five storeys high.

He raised the gadget into the air and pushed a button, causing the harpoon to soar towards the ceiling like a rocket, leaving behind a silver rope in its wake. The harpoon burst through the roof and hooked itself onto the edge of the freshly created hole.

"Are you sure it will hold?" I asked doubtfully.

"Of course," The Mystery replied. "I invented it."

He tugged on the rope twice.

"The M-Rope is secure," he said, attaching Mr Magic's unconscious body to the rope. He hooked an additional movable unit with handles to the gadget as well.

"This will bring us up, but the M-Rope can only support the weight of two people at a time. It can bring Mr Magic up last."

"Good enough," The Shock said, moving to hold the end of the rope steady. "Electric Boy and Pandora Girl first."

Pandora Girl deftly grabbed hold of the handles on the movable unit with both hands, and Electric Boy did the same from the other side of the rope. They were huddled close to each other, and he flashed a wide smile.

"You know, if the building wasn't on fire, this would actually be kind of fun," he commented.

The Mystery flicked a switch on the gadget, sending the movable unit all the way up the silver rope with its two passengers. They alighted on the roof without trouble, and The Mystery flicked the same switch again to bring back the movable unit.

"You and Lady Damage next," The Shock instructed The Mystery. The flames blazed around us, the heat and sweat misting my vision as The Mystery and Lady Damage ascended. When the movable unit returned, The Shock extended his hand towards me with a smile.

"Shall we?"

I wiped my forehead with the back of my glove, and then nodded and gripped the handles for dear life. The Shock flicked the switch, and the movable unit hurtled up to the roof with us in tow. It moved quicker than I had anticipated, making me half afraid of falling off into the fire.

Sensing the sudden jerk, The Shock's right arm instinctively fell around my waist, and he held me securely like a harness, making all my jitters of falling evaporate at once.

"So this is what it feels to fly," he said softly as the crackle of the fire faded, making me realise how close our bodies were.

Before I could reply, we had reached the roof, and the moment passed. The Mystery pushed a button from the harpoon end of his gadget and made the entire line retract upwards, bringing Mr Magic's body along with it like a fishing line.

The top of the building wasn't on fire, but that wouldn't matter if the burning building beneath us collapsed. The six of us sprinted across the rooftop to the edge of the building, The Shock carrying Mr Magic on his back. We used the M-Rope to rappel down to ground level again and didn't stop till we were a safe distance away from the blazing inferno.

"The police and fire department are on their way," The Mystery reported.

"Good job," The Shock said as he laid Mr Magic on the ground.

"We got what we came for," The Mystery said, taking out the wrapped object.

"Hopefully," Lady Damage added.

We gathered around The Mystery, who carefully untied the black cloth. It revealed a diamond that glowed in a bright purple hue. It looked beautiful...

"Looks like we really got it," Lady Damage sounded satisfied.

"It's bigger than I expected," I said.

"How is it glowing on its own?" Pandora Girl asked.

"More importantly, how does it give superpowers?" Lady Damage asked.

"Relax, girls," Electric Boy said. "The Mystery will figure it out."

"We'll study the Super Diamond in the Secret House," The Shock said. "If we find out how it gives superpowers, maybe we can come up with a way to remove them too. We must also find whoever gave the Super Diamond to Mr Magic and arrest him for aiding all the supervillains' crimes."

He reached out to hold the Super Diamond in his own hands. The diamond glowed a little brighter when it touched The Shock's bare skin, and I marvelled at the purple beams of light passing through the gaps between his fingers, only made more obvious by the darkness of the abandoned port at night.

"But even if we stop this one guy, Diamond City's supervillain plague still exists," The Shock continued, his voice hard. "The supervillains are getting more powerful and dangerous. We must end our supervillain plague *permanently*. Only then will Diamond City be truly safe."

IN THE NEAR FUTURE

"I did it, Mystery," The Shock said. "I found a way to end our supervillain plague."

The Shock grabbed The Mystery by the throat and threw him onto the ground.

"Do it, darling," Dream Girl's words cut through the air. "Kill The Mystery."

"No! Melanie!" I screamed.

"I told you," she glared at me. "Call me Dream Girl."

"What about the rest?" The Shock asked his lover.

"Kill them all," Dream Girl replied. "No more Super Secret."

#7

NORMAL IS BORING

"Help me get tickets to the next Secret Show!" Melanie tugged my arm. "There'll be *two* of the Super Secret appearing!"

"Where'd you hear that?"

"It's in this week's Super Addict Magazine! They have *inside* information. And if it's The Shock who is appearing with Electric Boy, then you *have* to get me in!"

"All the tickets are sold out. What makes you think I can get them now?"

"They were sold out the previous time, but you got them anyway! And you still haven't told me how you got them."

"I told you, it's a secret."

"Just tell me, Vee!"

"Alright, I'll help you get tickets again if you promise to stop asking me."

Melanie threw her arms around me. "I'm so lucky to have you as my friend! Maybe Electric Boy will appear with Pandora

Girl. Super Addict Magazine says the two of them are dating."

"Uh-huh."

"I doubt it'll be Lady Damage or The Mystery. They're both too cool for such a thing."

"Heh."

"It better not be Koolara."

I raised my eyebrows. "Why not?"

"She's so... normal."

"What's wrong with being normal?"

"Normal is boring! There's nothing interesting about Koolara."

"*I* think she's interesting. Her costume looks cool."

"You like her *costume*? She still hasn't told us why there're two arrows pointing up to her face, and she better not be dating The Shock or I'll-"

"She's *not*."

Melanie stared at me. "What makes you so sure?"

"Because..." I trailed off, wondering how I could steer the conversation to safer ground. I stopped short when we made a turn into a deserted alley and met a dead end. "Wait a minute," I blinked. "Did we cross the street at the junction just now?"

Melanie glanced around us. "I don't know. I was following you."

We had missed the last train for the day and were now going home by foot. I must have made a wrong turn somewhere and had been too sleepy to realise it. The late night air was freezing, and it was already dark out. Luckily, the streets of Diamond City were set ablaze by an army of street lamps. We would find our way back in no time.

"Never mind," I turned around. "Let's just go back and-"

I stopped when I saw that a dark silhouette had stopped behind us, blocking the alleyway. The figure was slightly taller than me and wore a hoodie over his head, his face masked in the shadows. He started closing in on us as soon as we noticed him.

"Vee, what do we do?" Melanie whispered.

"Stay close to me," I reached into my pocket for my phone, but he was already too close. He whipped out a knife and pointed it at us.

"Hands up!" he shouted roughly, unconcerned about being overheard.

Melanie shrank back, speechless, and hugged her bag tightly against her slim body. I took my hand out of my pocket and raised it slowly, eyes locked onto the knife's shiny blade.

"What do you want?" I asked.

"You'll see soon enough," the reply came from *behind* me. I whipped around to see the exact person standing there in the same outfit, grinning menacingly at us.

Melanie squeaked and jerked me closer to her. A third clone appeared on my left, twirling his knife expertly between his fingers.

"What's happening?" Melanie stuttered.

A new supervillain with superpowers? We may have acquired the Super Diamond from Mr Magic, but we didn't know how many supervillains had already gotten superpowers before that. There were at least five of the same hooded guy now, surrounding us from all directions. My fingers curled into fists, ready to defend myself and Melanie if any of them tried to strike.

The original one was still holding up his knife with a cocky smirk on his face. Maybe if I knocked him out, that would erase all his clones... but what if his superpowers didn't work that way? Could I fight all of them at once?

I could alert the Super Secret by pressing the secret button on my phone, but Melanie being here meant that I couldn't change into my Koolara costume. When my fellow superheroes arrive, they would only find two ordinary teenage girls…

The hooded guy seemed to be waiting expectantly for something to happen. He scanned the roofs of the building and cocked his ears to listen for some sign of movement but the quiet night disappointed him. He lowered the knife and pulled back his hood, revealing messy brown hair and haughty eyes.

"Looks like we need more than a simple robbery to draw him out," he drawled, his clones snickering from around us. "Let's have a little fun with these two sweet little-"

I rammed my foot into the guy's stomach like a sledgehammer, taking him by surprise and knocking him backwards. One of his clones tried to grab me from behind, but I spun around in time and swung my bag into the side of his face. My fist went straight for his chest, and my elbow connected with another clone's jaw from the side.

"Let me go!" Melanie screamed. She was caught in the arms of the hoodless original, who had recovered and was looking at me with that same annoying smirk. I cracked my knuckles, wanting nothing more than to punch it right off his face.

The knife came while I was distracted, its unseen blade slicing through my sleeve and into my arm. I cried as metal met flesh, and I swung wildly at my attacker, missing him completely. One of them swept me off my feet with a roundhouse kick, and I smashed into the brick wall behind me before slithering helplessly onto the wet ground. A shoe rested tauntingly on my injured limb and hatefully stomped, sending an avalanche of pain through my body. I screamed in agony as fresh blood seeped from my arm. It felt like my arm was being seared in two.

Darkness was creeping in from my peripherals as I struggled to stay conscious. I should have called for the Super Secret when I had the chance. I could have made up some story afterwards about how I found Koolara's phone and accidentally pressed the secret button, but it was too late now. I couldn't even tell what they had done to Melanie. This was all my fault-

"Hyuk!" one of the clones suddenly wobbled as if he were drunk. He fell to his knees and keeled over, unconscious. Around him, the clones started dropping one by one to the floor. The one nearest to me stumbled back, trying to find the unseen attacker, but he too halted, swayed for a moment and fell to the ground. As if the magic show had ended, every clone faded away into thin air before my eyes, leaving only the original behind.

He whipped around with Melanie in his grasp, holding the blade close to her face as he scanned the alley. Before he knew it, the weapon was sucked out of his hand and flung out of sight by an unseen force.

A shadowy figure appeared, his piercing red eyes illuminated by the moonlight above. He must have been moving so stealthily and fast that he managed to take out all the clones one after another and disarmed the original guy, all without being seen.

"You got superpowers from the Super Diamond," The Mystery's voice was as cold as the night.

"You can call me Shadow Hood," the guy responded. "I've wanted to meet you, Mystery."

Shadow Hood released Melanie, who stumbled in my direction and collapsed beside me. He raised his fists in a boxing stance, unafraid of the superhero in front of him. Melanie helped me sit up, stifling a nervous sob at my bleeding arm.

"Just a small scratch," I forced a smile. "Look, The Mystery's here. We're going to be okay."

"The police will arrive soon," The Mystery said. "And you will be going to Diamond Prison."

"Me?" Shadow Hood grinned. "Which one of me?"

An exact copy of him stepped out of his own body, and then a third emerged, all standing side by side like an army. It was quite a sight to behold, but the threat of such a supervillain set off alarm bells in my head. Who knows how many clones he could actually create?

"Tell me how the Super Diamond gave you superpowers," The Mystery said.

"In case it isn't obvious, I *outnumber* you, Mystery," Shadow Hood snorted. "So you better do as *I* say or I'll-"

He was knocked unconscious from the back by a mighty fist, and all his clones vanished once again. Melanie tugged my arm, fortunately, the good one.

"V-Violet..." she could barely form her words. "It's The Shock!"

"Is everyone alright?" The Shock asked, his eyes landing on me. "You're hurt..."

Both superheroes were already making their way towards me, and I didn't have the time or strength to react before The Mystery crouched down and carefully fixed a black cuff around my arm. I winced as the icy object wrapped around the open wound on my forearm like a metal bandage. I haven't seen this gadget before...

"Keep still," The Mystery looked up to address me. He caught my eye, and I shifted clumsily, hoping he wouldn't recognise me while Melanie stared unabashedly at the two teenage superheroes in front of us.

The Mystery tinkered with the gadget and pressed several beeping buttons. A thin layer of cold liquid seeped from the cuff, and I relaxed as it numbed the pain of the wound. The wound stopped bleeding, and I felt an odd, tingly sensation where the cuff was.

"The M-Ring will heal your wound completely," The Mystery said.

"Will this thing really heal her arm completely?" Melanie squeaked.

"Of course," The Mystery replied. "I invented it."

"You're going to be alright," The Shock smiled at me, and I tried to return the smile without making eye contact.

The metal ring around my arm suddenly snapped open, and I gasped quietly. Where the gash had been, new, raw pink skin had formed. It was as if I had never been cut! I tested my arm gingerly, and I could move it freely and painlessly again. The sinews and muscles had been fully healed. I wanted to thank The Mystery but feared he would recognise my voice.

The wail of police sirens blasted from the street outside, and then came the loud stomping of boots against pavement. A squad of policemen rushed onto the scene, carrying out the standard protocol that I had seen many times before.

"Please escort the two civilians back home," The Shock instructed. "I want them brought home safely."

"Will there be two of the Super Secret at the next Secret Show?" Melanie suddenly blurted, finally regaining enough nerve to ask her burning questions.

"Yes," The Shock flashed a confident smile. "I'll be appearing with Electric Boy."

"Oh, I submitted a question! By the way, my name is-"

"Melanie Mitchell," The Shock smiled. "You told me at Amazing Fashion, remember?"

"Y-you remember me?" Melanie tried to stand up, but her legs gave way. The Shock, ever chivalrous, caught her in time.

"Of course I remember you," The Shock looked into her eyes. "And your friend. How could I forget?"

I was almost certain that she would have swooned there and then had he not allowed the policemen to support her into the police car. "The Shock knows my name..." Melanie mumbled giddily.

Another two policemen came to help me up as well, but I stroked my upper arm, amazed that it had been perfectly healed by yet another one of The Mystery's amazing gadgets. Looking around, I realised that The Mystery was nowhere in sight.

The fight with Shadow Hood and his clones remained on my mind on the ride home. How many more supervillains with superpowers were there out there? Crime wasn't going to end in Diamond City, and I wished there was a way to rid the city of it once and for all. But for now, defending Diamond City alongside the Super Secret was the best that I could do.

NEXT TIME

KOOLARA MEETS DOCTOR GALAXY IN PRISON!

"I still can't believe The Shock knows my name."

"Me neither."

"Don't be jealous, Vee. There are boys who like you too."

"Uh-huh."

"Chris Campbell, for example."

"Chris? From Chemistry?"

"Yeah, he told me on the last day of school."

"And you never told me?"

"I thought he was joking! But then I remembered the way he always looked at you."

"He *never* looked at me."

"He looked at you *all* the time."

"No, he didn't… so, did he say anything else about me?"

"Hmm… I'll tell you if you get me tickets to the next Secret Show."

"I told you, I'm getting the tickets soon."

"The Secret Show is in two days' time! It's not like you know the Super Secret…"

#8

JEALOUS

"It's just a glowing purple rock," Lady Damage yawned, not keen on holding it any longer. "We've been tricked, guys."

We were gathered at the Secret House and were studying the Super Diamond for the past thirty minutes, which mostly meant passing it around while waiting for The Mystery to provide some answers. He was in his usual seat in front of the computer, typing away and producing tons of diagrams and numbers on the main monitor.

Lady Damage passed the purple rock along to The Shock with a shrug. Electric Boy was drumming his fingers on the table as he waited, occasionally stealing a glance at Pandora Girl, who was quietly swiping and tapping on her phone, absorbed in setting a new record for her game. The Shock held the Super Diamond and looked at The Mystery hopefully.

"Discovered anything?"

"I do not know how the Super Diamond gives superpowers," The Mystery replied, deadpan.

"Looks like we escaped a burning building for nothing,"

Lady Damage sighed.

"We *did* get the Super Diamond," The Shock said, finally putting it on the table that we were seated around. "That's a step in the right direction. If we know how it gives superpowers, maybe we can remove them too."

"I ran the Super Diamond through the M-Com using the highest scan settings," The Mystery said. "The construct of the diamond crystal is unlike anything I have seen before. Its crystal pattern has some similarities to the type of diamond which provides our power, but I need more time to do some tests and determine how it affects the human body."

"That's encouraging," Lady Damage said wryly.

"The Mystery has never failed us before," Electric Boy said. "You just have to invent a special something to decode it, or whatever..." he trailed off as The Mystery eyed him morosely.

"Is there anything else hidden inside the diamond?" I asked.

"No," The Mystery said. "I already scanned it five times."

"How is it glowing by itself?" Pandora Girl asked without looking up. A little victory tune tinkled from her phone, declaring her new high score.

"A strange chemical on the outer surface of the diamond is

reacting with the air around it and causing it to glow," The Mystery explained.

"I hate to be the one who asks this," Electric Boy sat up straight. "But is it edible?"

"I have something to say…" The Shock suddenly stood up. We all looked at him attentively.

"I think we should speak with the Supreme Court and propose to implement the capital punishment for all supervillains."

I pressed my fingers against the seat of my armchair during the awkward silence that followed.

"Capital punishment? As in, the death penalty?" Lady Damage asked.

"Yes, we should execute supervillains," The Shock said. "With the heaviest punishment in place, no one will even think of becoming a supervillain."

"Come on, we can't just *kill* anyone who puts on a weird outfit and attempts to rob a bank," Electric Boy laughed.

"We shouldn't execute someone for simply *being* a supervillain," Lady Damage said. "They should still be judged according to their crime."

"They're serving their time in Diamond Prison," Pandora Girl said. "They will learn to become better people."

"The fact that someone chooses to be a supervillain shows that he is pure evil," The Shock said firmly. "Maybe an ordinary criminal can change for the better, but supervillains will *never* change, no matter how long they stay in prison. You've seen what has happened in the past week. We need the most severe punishment in place to stop people from becoming supervillains in the first place."

"Capital punishment is much too severe," The Mystery injected. "There is no need to kill supervillains as a punishment."

"The law already has the death penalty for the most serious crimes such as murder or drug trafficking," The Shock said. "So why not have the same punishment for being a supervillain?"

Nobody had a response.

The Shock frowned as he turned to me. "Koolara?"

"Huh?" I gulped.

"What do you think?"

All eyes turned to me, and I kept my composure as I rested both arms on the table. The Super Secret was here to protect Diamond City from supervillains, and that has indeed worked well for the past year.

However, my mind drifted back to the fight with the Triple Dangers in Diamond South Bank, where The Shock slammed

Green Danger into the ground. I shuddered at how enraged The Shock had become in that moment.

They say *prevention is better than cure*, so maybe The Shock was right. Maybe we needed something *more* to stop people from becoming supervillains in the first place, but surely there had to be a better way...

"I agree with Mystery. I think the death penalty might be a little too drastic," I chose my words carefully. "Maybe we should think of other solutions before proposing capital punishment to the Supreme Court?"

"People can still commit crimes without being supervillains," The Mystery added. "They will be judged fairly by the law whether they are supervillains or not."

"But supervillains are inherently more *dangerous*," The Shock's voice became heated. "Don't you see? Their minds are only focused on harming the innocent for their own selfish gains..."

The phone rang, and Lady Damage picked it up with a coy "Hello". She listened for several moments, giving The Shock enough time to calm down.

"Yes, Sir, I'll tell him that," her eyes lit up hopefully. "Thank you very much."

She replaced the receiver with a renewed vigour.

"That was the Commissioner of Police," Lady Damage explained. "They've identified Mr Magic as Tyler Thompson. Time to do your thing, Mystery."

The Mystery typed the name into his computer and pulled up multiple articles relating to "Tyler Thompson", displaying them on the monitor. Not all of them were about the Tyler Thompson whom we were looking for. He scrolled through several of them before Pandora Girl gestured to stop.

"Look," she pointed to one of the newspaper articles which paraded the winners of the local science fair seven months ago. The picture featured two teenage boys, each posing proudly beside a familiar-looking flask of white goop. The caption read, "*TYLER THOMPSON AND PETER PINE BLOW JUDGES AWAY AT DIAMOND CITY ANNUAL SCIENCE FAIR.*"

Peter Pine… also known as Doctor Galaxy.

Looks like we have a lead.

DIAMOND PRISON

"Why did you volunteer to come?" I asked.

"Thought it'd be fun to see all our supervillains again," Lady Damage replied. "Don't be so uptight, Koolara. The Shock chose you! That means you're the best man, or *woman*, for the job."

"Sure," I said.

"How weird was he just now, right? I mean, a death penalty *would* deter people from becoming supervillains, but like The Mystery said, people can still commit crimes without being supervillains."

"I guess... but he did seem very determined to end supervillains permanently, especially with the supervillains getting actual superpowers from the Super Diamond."

"So, do you think the Super Diamond really came from Doctor Galaxy?"

"The Mystery said we can't be a hundred percent sure, so..."

"That's why we're here now."

"Yeah."

Lady Damage shifted in her seat awkwardly, an unusual gesture from her. She crossed one leg over the other and cleared her throat. "Did he say anything to you recently... about me?"

"Who?"

"The Mystery."

"Not really…"

"Nothing at all?"

I raised an eyebrow.

"What?" she said.

"You like The Mystery?"

"What? *No.*"

"Then why did you ask?"

Her slim fingers twirled a lock of her bright red hair. Melanie was right that Lady Damage looked even more gorgeous up close. She must have had an endless line of suitors in real life, but I wondered who could keep up with a girl who could leap six feet into the air or kick someone in the face effortlessly.

"Okay," she conceded. "I find him very… *intriguing.* He might seem like a cold person on the outside, but he's actually very sensitive."

"So, you like him?"

"I don't know… *maybe.*"

"Maybe yes, or maybe no?"

"Just maybe."

"Have you told him that you like him?"

"Of course not, are you crazy?" she stared at me wide-eyed. "But I don't think he likes me anyway. He spends way more time on his computer and microscope than me. How do you even know if a boy likes you?"

She's asking *me*?

"I don't know," I replied, actually feeling bad that I couldn't offer any good advice. "Maybe you can try asking him?"

"I've thought about asking him, but I've had so many bad experiences with boys before... they get tired of you easily. But The Mystery is different. The Mystery is dedicated. I've seen him work on something for days without stopping. If only he paid more attention to me. It *would* be nice if he and I..." she drifted off and sighed dreamily.

"Mm-hmm," I mumbled.

She shot me a look of warning.

"You can't tell *anyone*," she wagged a finger sternly.

"Relax, your secret is safe with me."

"It better be. I know your secret too."

"What secret?"

"You and The Shock."

"We are *not* dating... if, um, that was what you were going to say."

"Then why did you two lovebirds fight The SuperNova together?"

"He dialled me for help."

"He *only* dialled you for help."

"The rest of you were at the Secret House trying out The Mystery's M-Pills."

"Face it, he *likes* you."

"Where are people getting that idea!"

"It's obvious that he likes you a lot."

"Oh, really?"

"Yeah, I can tell from the way he always looks at you."

"He *never* looks at me."

"He looks at you *all* the time."

"He looks at all of you too."

"Come on, you know what I mean! And haven't you noticed that he always tries to sit next to you in the Secret House…"

"You notice a lot of things, don't you?"

Lady Damage laughed. "Maybe that's my superpower."

The door swung open and revealed the familiar figure we had been waiting for. He was dressed in the standard bright orange prison uniform, his wrists and ankles bound in metal chains that dragged noisily across the floor as he hobbled in.

"Doctor Galaxy," Lady Damage greeted him. "Please, have a seat."

He shuffled to the chair and sat, his cool green eyes surveying the two superheroes opposite him. His silky black hair was longer than I remembered, combed back and tucked behind his ears.

The media had heralded him as "Diamond City's deadliest supervillain". Some even argued that his sentence of two years was too short for all the destruction he had caused. After all, he was responsible for the partial collapse of several warehouses and causing harm to many innocent people.

I glanced the marks on his forearm which reflected the treatment of Paralysis Serum administered to all prisoners in the isolated "Supervillain Building" of Diamond Prison.

The Paralysis Serum was one of The Mystery's most brilliant inventions, used to deter supervillains from breaking out of Diamond Prison. If they went beyond prison boundaries, an elaborate tracking system would activate the serum, instantly numbing the necessary muscles required for movement, quite similarly to my stun darts. The Paralysis Serum would only be disabled by Diamond Prison at the end of the prisoner's sentence.

"Two beautiful girls visiting me in prison?" Doctor Galaxy sounded almost too relaxed for a prisoner. "What gives me the honour?"

"Thought it'd be fun to see our favourite supervillain again," Lady Damage said. "How's prison life?"

"Not bad," he replied nonchalantly. "Apparently, I have the best room in the building. The walls are a hundred percent impenetrable, and everyone knows my name. I'm like a celebrity."

"Good, because you have one and a half more years to enjoy that," Lady Damage smiled.

"That I do," he responded. "But that's not what you came down to talk about, is it?"

I glanced at Lady Damage from the corner of my eye, but I had nothing to worry about. She had everything under control.

"What do you know about the Super Diamond?" she asked, getting straight to the point.

The heavy chains around Doctor Galaxy's wrists clanged against one another as he placed his hands on the table. My own fists clenched under the table instinctively.

"I heard the Super Secret found Mr Magic's hideout at Diamond City Port and got it."

"So you *do* know about it," Lady Damage said.

"Word gets around… even in prison. We have television and radio too. You should join us sometime." He winked.

Lady Damage pulled out the Super Diamond and laid it on the table. It was now encapsulated inside a transparent casing made by The Mystery which seemed to stop it from glowing. A tiny frown crept onto Doctor Galaxy's face.

"Did you give this to Mr Magic?" Lady Damage asked.

His green eyes flickered to Lady Damage, and then to me, and then to the purple diamond resting between us. He thought carefully.

"Yes, I did," he finally said.

"Where did you get it?"

He pondered, but he remained quiet.

"How does it give someone superpowers?" Lady Damage continued.

Doctor Galaxy leaned back lazily in his chair with a smug look on his face. He knew something we didn't. He had the upper hand now, and he was enjoying it.

"I can tell you everything you want to know about the Super Diamond," he cracked a sly grin. "But on one condition…"

I held my breath as Doctor Galaxy leaned forward onto the table, the loud noise from the chains reminding us that we were talking to a deadly supervillain.

"I want to be released from Diamond Prison… *now*."

"I'm afraid we can't do that," I replied evenly. "All prisoners have to serve their full sentence, even celebrity prisoners."

His green eyes bore through me. "Don't you want to know how the Super Diamond works? I can tell you the secret of gaining *real* superpowers. The Super Secret will become more powerful than ever. You all will be *real* superheroes."

"Let me put it bluntly," Lady Damage interrupted. "The last time we met, you hurt innocent people and destroyed public property. You were trying to *kill* us. We can't let you go free like that."

Doctor Galaxy's eyes narrowed. We came here to find out how the Super Diamond granted superpowers, but…

"We don't negotiate with criminals, and we can't let you out," I said. "I'm sorry."

A sinister fire burned in his eyes as he looked into mine.

"You will be."

<u>NEXT TIME</u>

KOOLARA & ELECTRIC BOY TRAPPED TOGETHER!

"Super Addict Magazine has confirmed that Electric Boy is dating Pandora Girl."

"We've been through this a thousand times, Mels. It's all just speculation."

"But it could be true! I think it'll be super romantic if Electric Boy and Pandora Girl were really together. Don't you think they're a perfect match?"

"Uh-huh."

"Oh, have you gotten our tickets yet? The Secret Show is tomorrow, and I *cannot* miss The Shock!"

"Relax. I'll get the tickets."

"You better! The Shock and I have a special connection. It's like we were meant to be together."

"Uh-huh."

"I'm serious! I'll do anything to meet him again. Maybe I'll ask him if Electric Boy is really dating Pandora Girl."

"They don't know each other's real identities, Electric Boy said so."

"Yeah, but that doesn't mean they can't be dating each another or know who the others are dating. If only there was some way I could know for sure…"

#9

NOTHING HAPPENED

"I'm dating Dora."

"Huh?"

"No, what I meant to say was, I *dated* Dora. Actually, I wouldn't say I *dated* Dora. Did I say I was *dating* Dora? I didn't *date* Dora. I just went on *a* date with Dora. Am I saying Dora too many times?"

"Wait, what *are* you saying?" I was suddenly interested in what Electric Boy was rambling about. "You're dating Dora?"

"No."

"But you went on *a* date with her."

"Yes. I mean, I don't know."

"What do you mean, you don't know?"

"I went out with her, but it wasn't really a *date*. I mean, nothing happened."

"Nothing happened?"

"Nothing happened."

"Where did the two of you go?"

"The Secret House."

"What! That's the absolute worst place to bring a girl out on a date!"

"It *wasn't* a date! And what was I supposed to do? We can't be walking around in public in our costumes."

"Oh, you're right. So just tell her your real identity."

"That's ridiculous."

"Girls like honesty. She'll like you even more."

"I'm not sure she likes me in the first place."

"Come on, you're Electric Boy! Every girl likes you!"

"She probably hates me."

"But do you like her?"

"Yeah."

"Dora likes you too! Haven't you seen the way she always looks at you?"

"It's no use now, is it? We're going to die."

"We're *not* going to die! We're going to get out of here,

and you're going to tell her how you really feel!"

"Why are you shouting? I thought Koolara was supposed to be the quiet one!"

"Where did you read that? Super Addict Magazine?"

I wriggled violently in an attempt to loosen the ropes, but just like the previous hundred times I've tried, the ropes didn't give.

Electric Boy and I were tied to opposite sides of the same cylindrical pillar in standing positions. The last thing I remembered was making my way to Diamond Park to meet Electric Boy for the Secret Show tickets, but something in the air had smelt funny, and before I knew it, I had been out cold and woke up to this predicament.

The small room we were in was hot and stuffy, and beads of perspiration were rolling down the sides of my face. All the windows had been closed and taped up so that I couldn't even tell if it were night or day. I had absolutely no idea where we were.

"You know what I said to her?" Electric Boy sighed from behind the pillar. "If The Shock and I formed a duo, we could call ourselves *Electric Shock*. That's the best joke I could come up with, Koolara. It's not even funny."

"It's pretty good," I assured, looking around for some way

of escape. I couldn't even reach my phone to hit the emergency button. "Electric Shock would be so popular…"

"The funny thing is, we *were* going to appear together at the Secret Show tomorrow."

"Oh, that's right. The first Electric Shock!"

"Please stop saying that."

The door flung open for today's dramatic supervillain entrance. A sultry female who looked a little older than me strutted into the room like a runway model. She wore bright red lipstick, which matched the shade of her tantalising evening gown, and her hair resembled a tidal wave crashing down onto her shoulders. I had to admit that while her choice of outfit came across as non-functional, I admired her boldness and individuality.

"Do we know you?" I asked.

"You can call me Princess Poison," her voice was sweet and sharp, a razor dipped in honey. "And I thought *he* was the chatty one."

"He's in a bad mood," I said, giving her figure-hugging dress a quick once-over for any hidden weapons. "Or it might be that awful perfume you had that knocked us out. You should really consider getting some ventilation in here."

"Word is, you have some kind of magic diamond that

grants superpowers," Princess Poison purred, eyeing me. "Give it to me, and I'll let you both go."

"We still don't know how it works," I said.

"Doesn't matter. Give it to me, and maybe I'll tell you when I figure it out. Even if I can't, I can sell the thing to the highest bidder."

"I can't give it to you even if I wanted to. It's not with me."

"Then where is it?"

"With The Mystery."

"Get him to bring it here."

"I can call him," Electric Boy said from his side of the pillar. "Using my phone."

"Guess today's my lucky day," Princess Poison sneered as she circled round to Electric Boy. I couldn't see what was happening on the other side of the pillar, but Princess Poison sounded like she was enjoying herself.

"Let's see… oh, what else do we have here?"

"That's for Koolara."

"Ah, I almost forgot," Princess Poison showed me the two tiny slips of paper. "The next Secret Show is tomorrow, isn't it? I can't wait to see The Shock there too."

"Put the tickets back," Electric Boy said. "My phone is in my other pocket."

"What's the rush?" she said. A few moments passed before she made a satisfied "aha!"

"Be careful," Electric Boy said. "It's expensive."

"So, what's the password?"

"Koolara," Electric Boy said.

"What?" I responded.

"That's the password," Electric Boy said. "It's Koolara."

Princess Poison typed the word in, and her lips curled into a smile. "I must say, Pandora Girl would be extremely jealous if she knew you-"

A puff of black smoke shot out from the phone and engulfed her face in a thick dark cloud. She dropped the phone and shuffled backwards to avoid the smoke, but it wafted after her, clouding her vision. As she coughed uncontrollably and frantically tried to fan the smoke away, Electric Boy appeared in front of me with a tiny pocket knife in one hand.

"Knife in sleeve," he started to cut the ropes that bounded me. "Useful trick to have."

"You couldn't do that earlier?" I asked, keeping an eye on

Princess Poison.

"Hey, not everyone is as good with tricks as Mystery," he continued sawing. "I was trying to slip the knife out of my sleeve the entire time!"

The black cloud faded away, and Princess Poison was starting to regain her composure. I shook the cut ropes off and swung my fist at our captor, hoping to catch her off guard, but she dodged my attack and returned the favour with a jab. I ducked to the side, almost knocking into Electric Boy.

"Yikes! Be careful!" he yelped.

She lashed out at me again, but Electric Boy grabbed her arm and used her own momentum to throw her to the ground. She recovered with a scowl, her luscious hair now as messy as a bowl of spaghetti. I reached for my trusty K-Pistol, but Electric Boy gestured for me to wait.

The glamorously dressed supervillain was suddenly stumbling about, her hands stretched out in front of her as she tried to get her bearings.

"You-" she tried to speak, but then she fell forward and landed on her face.

"The stun smoke took a while to work," Electric Boy frowned. "Let's get out of here."

We dashed out into an empty street that I didn't recognise. Everything around us looked strangely clean and untouched. Even the building walls looked like they were painted yesterday.

"Where are we?" I asked.

"I think this is a newly developed area of Diamond City, somewhere on the east side," Electric Boy replied. "Don't worry. He'll be here any minute."

"He?" I repeated.

The fully masked superhero appeared next to me without warning, the red "M" across his chest glistening under the hot sun.

"Is he deadly?" The Mystery asked.

"*She*," Electric Boy gestured inside the building. "And no, she doesn't have superpowers. She just wanted the Super Diamond, but the stun smoke from my phone put her out."

"The police will be here soon," The Mystery said. "Wait outside."

His large black cape swept the floor behind him as he entered the building.

"Your phone has stun smoke now?" I asked.

"Yeah, but it really isn't a nice thing to have," Electric Boy replied. "Makes your phone heavier and makes you feel like you're carrying a *bomb* all the time, but I guess it did came in handy…"

"And *I'm* your password?" I crossed my arms.

"It's hard to guess!"

"Why not *Pandora Girl*? Since you're, you know, in love with her."

"She's the password if I wanted to use my phone as a normal phone. *Koolara* activates the stun smoke and sends a distress signal to The Mystery."

"I see. So are there any other gadgets hidden on you?"

"You've already seen the pocket knife, and um, my mask does something special as well, but I promised The Mystery not to tell anyone…"

"Your phone," The Mystery said, almost making me jump in shock. I didn't even realise he was back with us. He handed the phone to Electric Boy, who immediately pouted in despair.

"No! The screen is cracked!" he wailed.

"I can fix it," The Mystery said. "I can even reinforce the glass screen so it will not crack when dropped."

"Nah, it's okay," Electric Boy shook his head and pocketed the device. "I just want a normal phone from now on, but we should think of a way to activate my E-Bombs using voice control."

"I will work on it," The Mystery said, and then he turned to me. "Koolara, we need to talk about what happened yesterday."

"I already told you guys everything last night," I said. "Doctor Galaxy won't tell us how the Super Diamond works unless we release him from Diamond Prison."

"No, not about Doctor Galaxy. About The Shock going to the Supreme Court."

I shook my head, recalling the tense meeting last evening where The Shock revealed that he actually went to the Supreme Court by himself. They listened to what he had to say, but of course, adding a new law wasn't so simple. The last time our criminal law had a major change was more than a decade ago, and it seemed like there wasn't going to be another one anytime soon. Even if a new law was proposed, it would have to be approved by a string of committees and finally, the President herself. The whole process could take several years.

The Shock wanted us to go to the Supreme Court as the Super Secret. He believed that if it were the six of us together, then they would definitely be convinced and take action immediately.

We had refused to join his cause.

"I hope he'll forget about the whole thing," I said.

"Especially after we all were against it."

"He seemed particularly interested in your opinion," The Mystery said. "You do not agree with him, do you? If The Shock should try to change your mind…"

"He can't," I stated firmly. "I'm hoping *he'll* change his mind."

"Maybe the Secret Show tomorrow will help The Shock relax a little bit," Electric Boy said. "Anyway, you guys carry on without me. I have to prepare for tomorrow! Oh, before I forget, here are the tickets for you and your friend."

"Thanks a lot!" I took the precious tickets from him.

"You're most welcome," Electric Boy smiled. "This is going to be huge! We received *so* many questions, and you never know, The Shock might just shock everyone with his answers, no pun intended."

NEXT TIME

KOOLARA & THE SHOCK GET CLOSE!

"People are calling it the *Electric Shock*."

"Oh, really?"

"Yeah, and I heard they'll be selling Super Secret Stuff there. Do you think they'll sell the Shock hoodie?"

"Maybe."

"It's always sold out at Amazing Fashion! Why don't they make more?"

"They probably didn't expect it to sell out so fast."

"People are selling it online at insane prices."

"Don't worry, they're probably making more."

"Hey, you always manage to get Secret Show tickets even when they're sold out. Can you get a Shock hoodie for me too?"

"Umm… I doubt it."

"Oh well, at least we get to go to the Secret Show today. I wonder how many questions they'll be answering this time. Do you think The Shock will pick mine?"

"Maybe, if you're lucky."

"I'm sure he will. Don't forget, he knows my name!"

#10

SOMETHING SPECIAL

The crowd applauded thunderously, the group behind me still shouting at the top of their lungs. There were much more people in Diamond Park today, and I could tell that security had doubled. The huge outdoor stage with our group photo as the backdrop remained the same, but the presence of another Super Secret member, The Shock no less, made everything extra new.

"And the next question is from..." Electric Boy fiddled with his phone. "Maisy Monroe! And her question is *also* for The Shock! Hey, don't steal my show *that* fast!"

The crowd laughed. Melanie shifted her feet anxiously beside me, probably hoping for her question to be picked next. She was wearing her newly purchased Shock hoodie and was hoping that The Shock might notice her in it when he read her question... *if* he read her question.

"Maisy wants to know..." Electric Boy cleared his throat. *"If you could have any superpower, what would it be?* Wow, that's a really good question."

The audience started shouting suggestions. Flight,

teleportation, telepathy, invisibility…

The Shock chuckled and thought for a while.

"Superpowers should be used to protect the innocent," he said. "No matter what superpower I have, I'll use it to protect Diamond City."

"Oh, come on," Electric Boy put his hand on The Shock's shoulder. "Just pick one."

The Shock hesitated, but then answered. "I want the courage to be honest with those I care about, so they know how I truly feel."

The Shock's fans screamed enthusiastically in response. Beside me, Melanie was elbowing me in the ribs.

"He's *so* sensitive," she squealed.

"Looks like we only have time for one final question," Electric Boy said when the applause had faded. "And this lucky person was chosen specially by The Shock himself…"

Melanie squeezed my hand. *No* way, it couldn't really be-

"Melanie Mitchell," The Shock said. "I know you're here today."

Melanie yanked my arm so hard that I almost punched her on instinct.

"And her question is… oh, this is a good one," Electric Boy chuckled. *"What type of girl do you like?"*

A flood of murmurings and wolf whistles erupted from the crowd. Melanie squeezed my arm even tighter. The Shock turned to scan the crowd, and he somehow found us in the sea of faces.

"Good girls like you," he smiled.

LATER

My phone vibrated in a unique rhythm as we were walking out of Diamond Park. I scanned the screen and saw that The Shock had sent me a message.

"Who is it?" Melanie asked. "Your secret admirer?"

"I'm not as lucky as you," I joked, tilting the phone away so she couldn't see.

"Fine," Melanie said. "But I'll find out who your secret boyfriend is sooner or later, Violet!"

I forced a chuckle as I glanced down to read The Shock's text.

Koolara, come to Diamond Park at midnight. I want to show you something.

MIDNIGHT

I wondered if there was anyone else in Diamond Park now and how they would react if they saw an actual superhero. Maybe they'll think that I just came from a costume party.

My eyelids were getting heavier with each passing second, but the uncertainty of my situation kept me awake. I checked the text message again to make sure I read it right. What could The Shock want to show me? Melanie would *kill* to have a meeting with The Shock like this-

My train of thought snapped as my foot rammed into something hard. I tripped, but before I lost my balance completely, I felt a firm grip on my arm and was pulled back up, standing on both feet again.

"You really should watch your step, Koolara," a familiar voice greeted me. The Shock gently let go of my upper arm.

"Thanks," I kept my voice steady, using both hands to adjust my mask.

"Are you alright?" he asked.

"Yeah," I replied. "So, the Secret Show was a huge success, wasn't it?"

"Yes it was," he replied, glancing around us. His mind was obviously no longer on the Secret Show.

"I… want to show you something," he turned back to me. "If you promise not to trip over anything else."

I looked down to see a cunning tree root curling out and back again into the concrete pavement, barely visible in the darkness.

"I'll try my best," I smiled.

The Shock nodded as I followed him off the pathways and into the shadowy forest behind Diamond Park. It was a maze, but The Shock seemed to know where he was going. He constantly looked back to check that I was keeping up. I didn't keep track of how long we had been walking, but he eventually came to a halt.

"We're not in Diamond Park anymore," he announced.

I stopped, confused. We were in the middle of nowhere and only surrounded by more trees. The Shock took a few steps forward and carefully pushed aside a section of the thick foliage, revealing what looked like a… door? I gasped when I realised that we were in front of a small building camouflaged by the verdure growing around it.

"This is where I spend all my time," The Shock scratched the back of his neck sheepishly. He pushed a series of buttons on a small number pad located on the door, activating a string of clanging noises. It sounded like heavy bolts were being unlocked. The noises stopped and he pushed the door open.

The inside of the building was much bigger than it looked on the outside. Towering wooden shelves, filled with books of every kind, lined the four walls of the large square room, and stacks of newspapers and magazines cluttered the corners.

Stationery was neatly arranged on a table, and took me a moment to realise that the glossy magazine next to them was an issue of Super Addict Magazine. Funny how I'd never actually read this thing before. I didn't like to read about myself, much less what others thought about me.

"Sorry about all the papers," The Shock's voice made me jump. He appeared next to me, picking up stray newspapers from the ground and arranging them on the table. "You're the first person I ever brought here."

"You have a nice hideout," I looked around, still amazed by the amount of books in here.

"Oh, thanks," he scratched his neck again. "It's just another facility my parents built. Their new transport system was going to be huge... oh, take a seat wherever you like," he gestured for me to sit down.

Wherever was a choice between two armchairs placed side by side at the table. I plopped myself onto the nearest one and heard it creak under me. Glancing at the table, I put two and two together and realised that he was actually sorting out newspaper and magazine articles into scrapbooks. But what kind of information was The Shock storing here?

"So, what did you want to show me?" I asked.

The Shock sat next to me, his silky cape obediently flowing down one side of the chair. He opened a hefty hardcover book that was in front of us, revealing page after page of neatly clipped newspaper articles. They all seemed to bear a common theme.

"Are those all the articles about us?" I asked, catching glimpses of bold headlines and photographs as The Shock flipped through the book.

"Yes," he smiled proudly. "I saved every single one, even this."

He jumped to a page near the front of the book, showing me an article dated a year back with an image of the two of us standing side by side. The headline read, *"THE SHOCK AND KOOLARA, DIAMOND CITY'S SUPERHERO DUO!"*

Of course, that duo had since grown into a mighty six-member team.

"Can you believe it's only been a year?" he said. "So much has happened since we first started. We've defeated so many supervillains together."

"Yeah," I said. "We're going to need a bigger prison."

The Shock chuckled as he started flipping the pages again. "Do you remember the day we fought Doctor Galaxy?"

"Of course," I said. "It was last December."

"Correct," he stopped at an article with the headline, *"DIAMOND CITY'S DEADLIEST SUPERVILLAIN DOCTOR GALAXY DEFEATED BY THE SUPER SECRET!"*

There was a photo of Doctor Galaxy himself, decked in his flamboyant green costume, being escorted into a police vehicle, arms locked in a Secret-Cuff. There were at least ten policemen pointing guns at the supervillain.

"Here, read this," The Shock said.

I leaned in to read the text he pointed out. It was a description of Doctor Galaxy's weapons.

The Galaxy Ray, fired from Galaxy Cannons, is a highly concentrated form of an unidentified chemical. It is weaponised in a liquid state and is able to trap and immobilise any person upon contact. Prolonged exposure to high intensities of Galaxy Ray is known to disintegrate common materials such as wood and concrete.

Shivers ran down my spine as I remembered the destruction caused to Diamond City Port on that day. The police confiscated Doctor Galaxy's Galaxy Cannons, and they hadn't been seen again.

"Doctor Galaxy was no doubt the most dangerous supervillain we've faced," The Shock said. "But we worked well as a team to take him down."

"You were a great leader," I said.

"But still, the damage he did…" his face suddenly contorted with rage. "Innocent people were badly hurt. Public property was destroyed. If we hadn't arrived in time, things could've been far worse. What if Doctor Galaxy does something like that again after he's released?"

"Diamond Prison will give him time to reflect on his actions and change for the better," I said. "Isn't that the point?"

"He won't change for the better," The Shock scoffed. "None of them will. If they did, The SuperNova and the Triple Dangers wouldn't have turned to crime again. Our supervillain plague will never end unless we do something about it now. That's why we need a death penalty for supervillains."

His voice had reached a feverish pitch as it always did whenever he talked about something that he was passionate about. He turned to me hopefully.

"You'll support me, won't you?" he added. "You said that you didn't agree with me when we were discussing it in the Secret

House, but I know that was because the rest didn't agree, and you didn't dare to say how you feel. If the Super Secret's first two members agree on this, surely we can convince the rest too. Then the Super Secret can propose this to the Supreme Court and President Diamond..."

"But... I *don't* agree," I said slowly. "Supervillain or not, a criminal should be judged according to his crime."

"Supervillains are pure evil, and they will never change for the better. Why do we allow them to continue hurting innocent people?"

"The Super Secret is here to protect the people of Diamond City. We've been doing it for the past year."

"We can't be doing this forever, and we won't be so lucky every time we go out and fight crime. This is real life, Koolara, not a comic book. People can really get hurt in real life. People might *die*."

"Yes, I know people can get hurt in real life, I've seen it with my own eyes. But it's still not right to execute supervillains."

"Our law executes people for murder and drug trafficking. That's why people won't dare to do those things. Why can't we deal the same punishment to supervillains?"

"It's not our decision to make. We don't decide the law."

"We can at least propose this idea as a team. Maybe we can start a media campaign and get the public's support. I'm taking action before more people get hurt…"

"But the Super-"

"I'M DOING THIS TO PROTECT DIAMOND CITY!" The Shock slammed the table.

My heart skipped a beat at his outburst. I stared at him in stunned silence.

"I-" he looked away. "I'm sorry, so much has happened the past week…"

My mind went back to how he got wounded from fighting The SuperNova, how I had gotten injured from the fight with Shadow Hood and how more people had gotten hurt over the past week. I could see why he was so distressed over this issue.

I patted him lightly on the shoulder.

"Look, if you want…" I said. "We could go talk to the Super Secret together."

He looked up slowly and beamed. I liked how a simple smile from him could make people feel safe, like they had nothing to worry about if he was here. I returned the smile but froze when he reached for my hand. His fingers pressed the back of my glove, making my heart beat faster in an oddly ominous way.

"I'd love that," he smiled. "You can tell them that you agree with me, and then they will be convinced too."

He tightened his grip on my hand and locked his gaze on me. I was dumbfounded by what I was hearing. I realised that he might have misinterpreted what I said.

"What I meant was…" I gulped and shimmied out of his grasp. "We can discuss this with the Super Secret first, maybe work out other ways to deal with supervillains."

He blinked, and then his smile faded. "You still don't agree with me?"

"I…" I pressed my fingers against the seat of my armchair uncomfortably. "I don't think it's right to kill someone for simply being a supervillain."

"But…"

I stared at him. He wanted to say something, but the words wouldn't come out.

"But I thought-" he quivered in confusion, trying his best to keep his voice even. "I thought you liked hanging out with me and fighting supervillains with me, Koolara. You were the first to join my superhero team. You followed me *here*. I thought…"

He took a deep breath. "I thought you would support me because we had something special going on. I thought you liked me."

There, he said it. He thought I liked him.

What he was saying wasn't wholly untrue. I *did* like him and enjoyed hanging out with him, but definitely not in a *romantic* way. He had always simply been someone I looked up to, as a brother of sorts. I never knew that The Shock had hoped to be more than just friends. What was I supposed to say now? I've never had a guy say these things to me before. Everything was happening so fast. My palms were sweating. I gripped the armchair tighter. I needed more time to think…

He caught my hesitation. "You don't like me?"

"I do like you… only not like that. I'm sorry," I lowered my gaze and bit my lower lip. I felt terrible.

The Shock's face fell. He looked crushed. Even the diamond emblem on his chest seemed to have lost its sparkle.

"I thought that I was special to you too," he mumbled, more to himself than to me as he slowly got up from the chair.

He took something off one of the high shelves and held it up in his hand. It was the Super Diamond, but no longer in its casing.

I slowly rose from my seat, keeping my eye on the Super Diamond but unsure of what The Shock was planning to do. Had he figured out how it gives superpowers? No, he would have told us if he did...

"I've been spending a lot of time with the Super Diamond," his voice taut. "Have you ever held it in your hands? I mean, without the gloves, so you can really *feel* it. No, none of you have. I'm the only one who has felt its real *power*."

My body tensed up as I watched the Super Diamond glow more ferociously in The Shock's bare hands.

"What's happening to it?" I looked at The Shock. "Why is it glowing so-"

The entire room was suddenly engulfed by a blinding light. A relentless force hurled me backwards into one of the bookshelves. My head slammed against solid wood. The impact knocked all the wind out of me, and I dropped heavily to the ground.

And then everything turned into pitch darkness.

NEXT TIME

DAISY DIAMOND?

"Do you think the Super Secret has a secret headquarters?"

"Secret headquarters? Like a Batcave?"

"Yeah, and I bet they have those gigantic screens for spying on people."

"That only exists in movies, Mels. There's no such thing in real life."

"Then how do they always know where all the crimes are happening?"

"They probably have a telephone that the police can call them on."

"Telephone? What makes you say that?"

"I watch Batman too."

"Ha. But it would be cool if they had their own superhero vehicle, like a Batmobile."

"The Super Secret likes to do things quick and clean. A vehicle would look cool but is an unnecessary hassle and not to mention, super expensive to maintain."

"Wow, Vee, for someone who usually doesn't care, you've really thought it through. Maybe they should hire you as their super butler…"

#11

JUST BEING NICE

"Koolara…"

Someone was nudging at my shoulder.

"Can you hear me?"

Was that Lady Damage?

I opened my eyes slowly and pushed myself up into a sitting position, feeling my strength gradually returning to me. My fingers instinctively reached for my mask, making sure that it was still there.

"Are you alright?"

Lady Damage was kneeling in front me. I caught a whiff of her perfume, which almost made me sneeze.

"Where am I?" I said. My throat was dry. "What-"

"Can you remember what happened?" Lady Damage asked.

"She needs a little more time to recover," a familiar voice said.

The Mystery was here too?

He was at one of the many bookshelves, glancing through each book methodically.

"We found you using the M-Tracker," Lady Damage held up a familiar gadget with three knobs, the screen blinking with purple digits. "You remember the red pill that Mystery made us all swallow? It actually works!"

"Of course it works," The Mystery reached out to retrieve his gadget. "I invented it."

I had regained most of my strength by now. I stood up and felt a million pins and needles poking my feet, an analogy that really wasn't far off. I walked towards the table and sat in the same armchair, hearing it creak under me again.

"You should be back to normal now," The Mystery said, consulting the M-Tracker.

"Okay, so now that you're normal again," Lady Damage looked at me. "What are you doing in this tiny building in the middle of the forest?"

Building! Forest! I suddenly remembered what happened.

"The Shock!" I exclaimed. "We have to find him!"

"What happened?" Lady Damage asked, looking bewildered.

"The Shock brought me here," I spoke urgently. "He still thinks we should execute supervillains. He tried to convince me to support him."

"Where is The Shock now?" The Mystery asked.

"I don't know," I replied. "He had the Super Diamond, but he had taken it out of the case you made. He was holding it and it was glowing brighter and brighter, and then there was an explosion! I was thrown backwards and knocked out."

"I discovered that the Super Diamond has a very special reaction with human skin," The Mystery said calmly. "The Shock must have been holding the Super Diamond in his bare hands for too long. The chemicals in the diamond became unstable and eventually caused an explosion."

"The Shock brought the Super Diamond here?" Lady Damage couldn't believe it. "What was he trying to do with it?"

"We need to find him," I said. "I didn't see what happened to him after the explosion. He might be hurt."

No need to tell them what else happened here.

"He is not on my M-Tracker," The Mystery brought our attention to the device in his hand, which displayed "THE SHOCK" and "INACTIVE" in bold letters.

"Of course he isn't," Lady Damage said. "The M-Tracker

only detects you if your heart rate goes *under* or *above* the regular human heart rate. The tracker essence would wear off too quickly if it was active inside you twenty-four hours a day."

The Mystery and I stared at her.

"That's…" Lady Damage twirled a lock of her hair. "That's what you told me before we came here."

"Correct," The Mystery said. "Unless his heart rate goes out of the normal human range, there is no way we can track him."

I sighed, also realising that if that was how the M-Tracker detected you, then the blast from the Super Diamond must have hit me really hard-

A loud clang erupted from the door. Someone was trying to get in. Lady Damage took a step forward, but The Mystery pulled her back. I gathered my wits about me and fell into my combat stance, not knowing what to expect. Had The Shock returned?

The door swung open, revealing a familiar figure whom I recognised immediately. It was Daisy Diamond, the President's daughter, but instead of the friendly, happy fan at the Secret Show, her face was twisted with blind rage. She was charging straight toward us, a blazing fire in her eyes.

"Daisy?!" Lady Damage exclaimed, startled and confused.

Daisy made no sign of recognition. Instead, she gestured

with open palms, and a mini cyclone knocked us all away at the same time. I was thrown backwards by the unexpected force, crying out in pain as my hip slammed into the table behind me.

"She has superpowers," The Mystery hollered over the rushing winds. "Pin her down!"

Daisy splayed her fingers in The Mystery's direction, sending him flying into the nearest shelf, the books plummeting to the ground. Lady Damage swung her L-Whip towards Daisy, but it was blown away by the intense winds, never reaching its target. Lady Damage circled around instead, grabbing Daisy from behind with both arms and giving two short kicks to the back of her knees, making her stumble forward.

"Daisy, stop it!" she yelled, holding Daisy in her grasp.

I aimed my K-Pistol at Daisy, but a torrent of books came crashing into me and knocked me down. Daisy wrestled like a wild animal, elbowing Lady Damage sharply in the stomach and causing her to lose grip. Lady Damage recovered quickly and tried to pin her again, but Daisy waved her fingers, whirling Lady Damage away in a strong vortex. She smashed heavily into the table and disappeared behind the overturned chairs.

I kept low and crawled to where they were, trying to get a better shot. Another vortex of books came at me, and I rolled deftly to the left, narrowly missing several hits. I squinted and took a shot at Daisy, but in the whirling debris, the stun dart never made it to her.

To my horror, the table at the centre of the room was also starting to move with the strong winds. Daisy shot out her hand, and the entire table suddenly lunged straight at me. I knew that it was probably too late to dodge the oncoming large object, so I crouched down and used both my arms as a shield. The table, however, altered its course at the last second and flew past my right shoulder, missing me cleanly. The Mystery had used his M-Rope to pull the table away from me. I noticed that Lady Damage was already behind Daisy with her L-Flash in hand.

"Daisy!" she called out again, and as soon as Daisy turned towards her, she activated the red blast of light.

Daisy yelled as the light blinded her, and Lady Damage delivered a low sweeping kick aimed at her ankles. Daisy went down with a cry. Lady Damage hopped on top of her, trying to pin her down as she struggled violently, flaying her limbs as if she were drowning. The effect was chaotic. Books shot around like bullets and stray sheets circled the air. It was like being inside a hurricane.

"Hold her steady!" The Mystery said, his voice distorted by the gushing wind.

I got hit by several flying books as I clambered to Daisy's

side. With Lady Damage's help, we managed to pin Daisy's arms firmly to the floor. The Mystery came close and reached for Daisy's head, swiftly but carefully removing a tiny object from her temple. Daisy gradually stopped convulsing, the swirling winds in the room dying down with her. I gradually let go of her arm.

"What happened to her?" Lady Damage asked shakily, releasing Daisy. "What was that thing on her head?"

The Mystery held up a flat, square-shaped computer chip with exposed circuitry. He turned it over carefully with two fingers.

"This is a CMCU, Cybernetic Mind Control Unit, originally created by Diamond Prison to keep their most dangerous prisoners under control. However, they drained the wearer's energy too quickly and left them in a critical condition after a few hours, so the government banned the CMCU project and is using my Paralysis Serum instead."

He glanced at Daisy. "Daisy Diamond was manipulated by somebody to attack us. Her body has been weakened drastically by the CMCU, but I removed it just in time before-"

"Uugh!" Daisy choked, stirring slightly.

"Help her up," The Mystery said.

We pulled her up into a sitting position. Her face was as

white as a sheet and her lips were dried and cracked. She tried to move, but her body was void of energy. Lady Damage kneeled in front of her, but she spoke first.

"Lady Damage," she smiled weakly, barely able to speak. "You were always my favourite."

"You're just being nice," Lady Damage said softly, taking in the heart-shaped necklace that bore the initials "L.D." around Daisy's neck.

"Do… you remember me?"

"Of course I remember you, Daisy," Lady Damage assured warmly. "We sat next to each other in class for a whole year."

A tiny smile crept onto Daisy's lips. "Remember that cute guy… in the front row?"

"The one who had three dogs?" Lady Damage chuckled. "What was his name? Mike?"

Daisy nodded slightly. "He's my boyfriend now."

"You're kidding."

She shook her head. "He likes my purple hair."

"Guys are weird."

"You always had more."

Lady Damage laughed a watery laugh and squeezed her hand. "But you got the best."

She turned to The Mystery, a single tear glistening down her mask. "Is she going to be okay?"

"I already called for help," The Mystery said. "She will be fine."

"I'm sorry I attacked you," Daisy whispered. "I had no choice. He was controlling me from his device... I tried to fight it, but I couldn't..."

"Who was controlling you?" Lady Damage asked, leaning in to listen.

Daisy shut her eyes, as though the memory pained her.

"Doctor Galaxy," she opened her eyes. "He has superpowers... teleportation. He appeared in my room and stuck that thing on me. He gave me superpowers using the Super Diamond..."

"From the what?" Lady Damage said. "But that means..."

"The Shock-" I muttered.

"That is how he knew where this place is," The Mystery said. "Where we would be."

"He made me come here to deliver a message..." Daisy

said, taking slow breaths. "He wants the Super Secret to be at Diamond Central Street tomorrow at noon."

She clutched Lady Damage. "You have to stop him…"

We heard the sound of the police approaching the building, and a group of medics came rushing in, shouting for a stretcher and other equipment.

"You're going to be okay," Lady Damage said, giving Daisy's hand one last squeeze as she was helped onto the stretcher.

"You must stop him…"

"I promise you," Lady Damage said. "We will."

NEXT TIME

THE SUPER SECRET VS DOCTOR GALAXY!

"Our supervillains are always robbing banks and museums and the same old stuff like that. What if they do something more epic one day?"

"This is real life, Melanie, not some Hollywood movie."

"Even if a supervillain did something epic, I bet the Super Secret could handle it. The Shock is *invincible*."

"You know The Shock is just a normal human being, right? He doesn't have any superpowers."

"How would you know? Haven't you seen those supervillains with superpowers?"

"Yeah, but the Super Secret doesn't have actual superpowers. They rely on their combat skills and high-tech gadgets to fight supervillains."

"You always seem to know a lot about the Super Secret, but you never get excited when you actually meet them."

"Meeting them is rarely a good thing. Remember the two times we got close to The Shock? We could've been seriously hurt."

"But we turned out alright, didn't we? Hey, maybe *we* should be superheroes!"

#12

DREAM GIRL

"The people have been evacuated," the police squad leader reported. "We've checked all the shops again. There're no more news crews hiding around."

"Good," The Mystery said. "Guard the junctions that lead here so no one wanders over. Make sure the people are safe. Go, now."

The squad leader gave a firm nod, and his team rushed off in various directions, leaving the five of us in the deserted street. For the first time in history, Diamond Central Street was dead silent, pregnant with anticipation. All my senses were focused in the new quiet, watching and waiting for any sign of Doctor Galaxy.

"Why are we standing out in the open like this?" Electric Boy grumbled, but I could tell that he was nervous. "We're sitting ducks!"

"We have to show him that we are here," The Mystery said.

"We don't have to play by his rules," I said. "We're the good guys!"

"Stay alert,' Lady Damage said. "It's noon."

"Over there!" Pandora Girl was pointing at something down the street, about a block away.

A cloud of green smoke had started to form in mid-air, and we watched as a familiar character appeared within the mist. Doctor Galaxy sported the same dark green fabric, the tight long sleeves and boots with leather straps, his ensemble reminding me of the terror he caused at Diamond City Port six months ago. He wielded two golden Galaxy Cannons that were attached to his arms, and I suppressed all the fear that was bubbling up inside me.

"The moment we've all been waiting for is here!" Doctor Galaxy's words echoed down Diamond Central Street. "The Super Secret versus Doctor Galaxy, round two!"

"We defeated you the last time, and we'll gladly do it again," Lady Damage said.

"That's what you promised your friend, Daisy Diamond, isn't it?" Doctor Galaxy grinned.

Lady Damage took a quick step forward, but The Mystery made a sharp noise under his breath for her to stand down. We had no idea what new tricks Doctor Galaxy had hidden up his sleeves, but we were about to find out.

"It's too bad you won't be able to keep that promise,"

Doctor Galaxy continued. "Because this time, I brought along my secret weapon…"

A new cloud of smoke materialised around him, again glowing in a dazzling shade of green. When the thick cloud vanished, my body went cold.

"You made the best decision of your life," Doctor Galaxy laid a hand on The Shock's broad shoulder. He looked almost too tiny beside The Shock's mighty frame. "Who needs your puny friends when you can join *me*?"

My attention had been so focused on The Shock that it took me a few moments to register who the girl beside him was. She stood next to The Shock in her stilettos, mini skirt and Shock hoodie. Her hair was long and silky, falling down the sides of her face like elegant waterfalls.

No, it couldn't be… this must be some kind of illusion… there was no way that-

"Do it, darling," Melanie spoke, striking a pose with her hands on her waist. The Shock hoodie that was left unzipped showed off her slim figure perfectly, and she did look very convincing as The Shock's sidekick, but… how?

The Shock brushed Doctor Galaxy's hand off his shoulder with a single swipe. He turned to face Doctor Galaxy with a grim expression on his face, towering over him and making him freeze in fear.

He grabbed Doctor Galaxy by the arm and twisted it behind his back. His other hand reached forward and yanked the Galaxy Cannon right off Doctor Galaxy's arm where it had been strapped, the broken cords dangling uselessly from his wrists. Doctor Galaxy turned to fire his other cannon at The Shock, hitting him squarely with a stream of Galaxy Ray, but The Shock was unfazed. He smirked as the bright liquid trickled off his diamond crest harmlessly. Doctor Galaxy paled.

"No-" Doctor Galaxy stuttered in disbelief. "You can't-"

"Sorry, but I promised the people that I'd use my superpowers to protect Diamond City," The Shock said.

The Shock blasted Doctor Galaxy with his newly-acquired Galaxy Cannon. The Galaxy Ray swallowed Doctor Galaxy's torso, encroaching onto his neck and his arms and disabling his movements almost instantly.

"How?" Doctor Galaxy scowled, unable to break free from the Galaxy Ray's hold. "I was controlling you!"

"Oh, with *this*?" The Shock peeled off the small metallic square object from his temple. "You thought you could control me with this thing? The Super Diamond gave me *invincibility*, and that includes my *mind*. Nothing can control me."

"Did The Shock say he's invincible?" Electric Boy echoed.

"What do we do?" Pandora Girl asked.

We instinctively turned to The Mystery for the plan, but he hesitated with the latest turn of events. Perhaps for the first time in history, The Mystery didn't have a plan.

"Don't bother trying to teleport away," The Shock smiled at Doctor Galaxy, twirling the cannon easily in his hands. "Your very own Galaxy Ray is keeping your body right here, and there's no way you can break free of it."

The Galaxy Ray had completely immobilized Doctor Galaxy like a gooey straitjacket, and he was now at the mercy of The Shock. Doctor Galaxy glanced at us, panicked. His desperate gaze was pleading for help, begging us to intervene and save him…

"Mystery!" Lady Damage hissed, alarmed and impatient at The Mystery's lack of direction. I swallowed and waited for The Mystery to give some kind of signal, but he held his ground and remained silent, watching the series of events unfold before his eyes.

"Nothing can save you now," The Shock said, glaring at Doctor Galaxy. "You have brought much destruction to Diamond City and even blackmailed us into giving you freedom. For being a supervillain, you must pay the price."

Without warning, The Shock went for Doctor Galaxy's throat, gripping so tightly that Doctor Galaxy choked in horror. His body writhed under the Galaxy Ray, but he still couldn't move to loosen The Shock's chokehold on him. My blood ran cold as I saw the supervillain thrash about, but then The Shock released him, letting his unconscious body crumple to the ground.

"But not today," The Shock continued. He looked at Melanie, who had been watching all of it, amused. "We shall have a public execution to show the people of Diamond City what happens to supervillains from now on. If the law won't do it, then I'll kill all supervillains myself."

"Did he say… *kill?*" Pandora Girl murmured.

"Okay, seriously, what's the plan?" Lady Damage snapped.

The Mystery whipped out a gadget shaped like a shotgun, gripping its handle tightly with one hand and the long barrel with the other.

"Get behind me," he said.

"A *gun?*" The Shock chuckled mockingly. "I know how to get superpowers from the Super Diamond, and it's actually pretty simple. You just have to *touch* it long enough! We all can get *real* superpowers and use them to the best of our capabilities. We can protect Diamond City like *real* superheroes!"

"You need to stop what you are doing," The Mystery aimed his weapon at The Shock. "We are superheroes. We defend the law, not execute it. Our job is to bring supervillains to court, not condemn them to die."

"There will be absolutely *no* crime in this city because of the Super Secret," The Shock said. "We will punish anyone who stands in our way, just like how I'm going to get rid of our deadliest enemy Doctor Galaxy!"

"You do not know what you are saying," The Mystery tried again. "Superheroes do not have the right to kill. That is not what superpowers are for."

"A real superhero does whatever it takes to protect his city," The Shock gritted his teeth. "If you're not with me, then you're against me, so choose wisely, Mystery. I don't like people in my way, especially *you*."

He gripped the Galaxy Cannon forcefully, and his eyes glinted as he marched towards us, his every step setting off tremors in my heart. I clenched my fists and hoped that this didn't have to end in a fight, a hope that was quickly diminishing by the second.

"Stop it now, Shock," The Mystery cocked the gun.

"Or what? You'll shoot me?" The Shock laughed. "What's that gun going to do, make me dizzy?"

The Mystery pulled the trigger and released a blast of black energy which sizzled through the air. Whatever it was, it was useless. The blast hit The Shock and quickly dissipated. The Mystery fired several more times, but The Shock was impenetrable. The Mystery dropped the weapon and whipped out a handful of darts, flinging them towards The Shock expertly. The darts bounced off The Shock and dropped to the floor like flies. The Mystery hurled a second barrage of darts, and then a third, but nothing was working. The Shock wore a smug look as he continued advancing toward us.

The Mystery reached behind his back for yet another weapon, but then he hesitated.

"Get out of Diamond Central Street," he told us. "I will stop The Shock."

The four of us exchanged quick glances. We had always been a team, and that wasn't going to change, even if that team was now five instead of six.

"Too bad," Lady Damage said. "We're staying with you."

The Shock was only several paces away from us now and had raised the Galaxy Cannon, aiming it at The Mystery. The expression on his face was unlike anything that I'd ever seen...

He was about to fire when a blurred hand knocked the Galaxy Cannon away. Electric Boy had manoeuvred past The

Mystery and was now standing defiantly in front of The Shock. The height difference between the two was apparent, with The Shock towering inches above Electric Boy, but Electric Boy wasn't scared.

"Out of my way," The Shock instructed.

"Or what?" Electric Boy responded fearlessly.

The Shock chuckled to himself, amused, and fired a shot of Galaxy Ray at Electric Boy.

Pandora Girl screamed and dashed forward. Lady Damage and I sprinted after her. We heard The Mystery call for us to stop, but it was already too late.

I couldn't see what tripped me, but I fell to the ground and grimaced in pain, the rough road scraping my knees. I tried to get up, but an invisible force was pushing me back down. It felt as if someone had dropped giant weights on my shoulders.

I could still move my head, but what I saw wasn't good. Pandora Girl, Lady Damage and The Mystery were also pinned to the ground, fighting against the same unknown power that was keeping us all immobile. Meanwhile, The Galaxy Ray had already inched across Electric Boy's torso, covering most of it and locking him in position.

"Hmm," The Shock turned to Melanie, who was still

standing some distance behind him. "Thank you, my love."

Melanie had both her arms stretched towards us, a sly grin plastered across her face.

"Is the girl doing this?" Lady Damage asked, still trying to break free.

"Yes," The Mystery answered. "She seems to be capable of telekinesis."

"I can't get up…" Pandora Girl struggled where she was.

Melanie has superpowers too?

"Don't worry," The Shock added, slowly turning back to Electric Boy. "I'll make this one quick."

"What's wrong with you, Shock?" Lady Damage yelled.

"Don't hurt him!" Pandora Girl screamed.

"Let him go!" I cried, but The Shock ignored us.

"Fine, I'll let you have your own Secret Show, okay?" Electric Boy laughed, although he failed to break free of the Galaxy Ray's hold. "And just so you know, I was the one who started those rumours about you and Koolara. I could tell that you had a thing for her, so I let it slip that you two were dating. I just wanted to see how people would react if two of the Super Secret were a couple, and it turns out, it's actually not that bad."

The Shock had reddened, annoyed. "Why would you do that?"

"Because I wanted to be with Pandora Girl," Electric Boy said. "But I was scared of being in a relationship, especially a public relationship. I was scared of how other people might see me and whether my fans would continue rooting for me. But you know what? Now that I'm here, I realise I don't care about all that. Those aren't important. Being with Dora is, and I missed my chance just because I'd worried too much..."

My head was spinning. Was he saying all this as a trick? To stall for time? No, it wasn't just a show... he was telling the truth.

"And why are you saying this now?" The Shock frowned.

"I'm going to die now, aren't I?" Electric Boy chuckled. "Might as well tell Dora how I really feel..."

He still couldn't move his body, but he managed to turn his head enough to glance at Pandora Girl, who had tears streaming down her cheeks.

"I'm sorry," he said. "For bothering you."

"Don't be stupid," Pandora Girl said. "I want to be with you too, and I don't care what other people think."

The Shock suddenly threw his Galaxy Cannon violently onto the ground such that it cracked into half.

"Did you mean it?" he stared at Electric Boy. "What you said about wanting to be with Pandora Girl?"

"Every word," Electric Boy replied calmly.

"Then join me," The Shock offered. "You can be with her forever. I'd make sure of it."

Electric Boy held his unwavering gaze and shook his head slowly.

"No," he said. "I'm not joining you in killing people. In fact, I will do everything I can to stop you."

The Shock hardened again, his cool, arrogant exterior gliding back in place.

"Nothing can stop me," he responded.

Still gripping Electric Boy by the wrist, he lunged for Electric Boy's throat, and there was nothing that we could do except watch in horror. Electric Boy strained against The Shock's grip to look at Pandora Girl again.

"It's okay…" his lips trembled, forcing his cocksure grin, and perhaps for the first time in history, I paid full attention to what Electric Boy had to say.

"The Mystery will figure it out."

The Shock's grasp tightened, and within seconds, Electric

Boy crumpled onto the ground, motionless. The stunned silence that followed only made the blood pounding in my ears too loud. Pandora Girl had buried her face in her arms. Lady Damage had her back hunched over in despair. No sarcastic comments. No wisecracks.

"Electric Boy will die in the public execution as well," The Shock said. "Together with Doctor Galaxy."

"Why?" The Mystery growled. "He did nothing to you."

"Precisely," The Shock replied, dusting his hands with a satisfied look on his face. "What good is he if he does *nothing*? All he does and talks about are his stupid Secret Shows. We shouldn't need to put on circus acts to make our living. We are superheroes, and the city owes us. If you're not going to join me, then you will suffer the same fate as him."

My jaw dropped. I couldn't believe the words that were coming from The Shock, the superhero who inspired me to become one myself.

"You wished it were true," The Mystery murmured quietly.

The Shock stared at him, his eyes narrowing. "What?"

"You did not debunk the rumour," The Mystery continued. "You wanted it to be true. You wanted to be with Koolara."

I gulped at the mention of my name.

"You don't *know* me," The Shock hissed. "You'll never understand how I feel. Do you even *feel* anything under that mask, Mystery? Do you know what it's like to never get what you want?!"

The Mystery flinched. "I have feelings like any other human being, but they do not result in actions which harm my friends."

"I'm doing whatever it takes to protect my city," The Shock smiled crookedly. "I'm not the bad guy."

The Shock was eyeing The Mystery ominously, and I knew that I had to do something before anyone else get hurts. I had to at least try.

"Shock!" I called from the ground, hoping that I was doing the right thing.

The Shock turned to me.

"If… if I go out with you…" I said, trying my best to stop my teeth from chattering. "Will you stop all this?"

The Shock looked unimpressed with my offer.

"Oh, Koolara…" he laughed quietly. "I'm *over* you. Can't you see, I've found a girl who truly loves me."

I cringed and felt my cheeks getting hot. What was I thinking? I shouldn't have said anything in the first place! Melanie still had her arms outstretched towards us, pinning us to the ground.

"*She's* my Dream Girl," The Shock proclaimed. "She's beautiful, obedient *and* she loves me. What more could I ask for?"

He ran his fingers through his hair and strolled towards The Mystery, staring down at him with a cunning smirk.

"I did it, Mystery. I found a way to end our supervillain plague."

The Shock grabbed The Mystery by the throat and lifted him up. The Mystery grasped at the arm that was choking him, but The Shock was unstoppable. The Shock threw him hard onto the ground, causing The Mystery to groan in pain. I cringed and turned away, too horrified to look.

"Join me, Mystery," The Shock said. "We can protect Diamond City like real superheroes."

The Mystery struggled to stand, his legs failing to support him.

"No," he said firmly, struggling from the ground. "Superheroes do not kill."

Melanie came beside The Shock and looped her arm through his.

"Do it, darling. Kill The Mystery."

"No! Melanie!" I cried desperately.

She looked at me and frowned.

"I told you, call me Dream Girl."

She didn't know who I was... she didn't know that Violet was Koolara!

"What about the rest?" The Shock asked his lover.

Dream Girl surveyed the scene and shrugged. "Kill them all. No more Super Secret."

The Shock smiled, his gaze sweeping over all of us. "All of you will join the public execution, if it makes my girl happy."

"This is not you, Shock!" I yelled. "The Shock I know would never kill anyone!"

"Hmm," he stared at me. "Then why not I kill one of you *now* to show that I'm serious..."

He launched his fist at The Mystery's stomach.

I realised that Melanie was no longer holding out her hands towards us, and the force that had been pinning us down had already been lifted. It seemed to have dawned onto Lady Damage and Pandora Girl as well, because they immediately rushed in to fight The Shock, unleashing their weapons in full force. I wanted to join them, but I saw Melanie approaching from the corner of my eye.

"Melanie, stop it!" I yelled, arming my K-Pistol.

She flicked her hand and whipped the K-Pistol right out of my grasp with ease. Thrusting her arm forward, she caught me in her invisible grip. My body was not mine to control anymore. I was as stiff as a board, straining and failing to move my limbs.

"The Shock loves *me*, not you!" she spat, glaring at me as if she hated me. All at once, I remembered the rumours that she had read about Koolara and The Shock and realised why.

"How can you do this?" I said. "How can you agree to kill people?"

"I do whatever The Shock wants me to do!" she said, sending me flying towards the pavement with a sweep of her hand. I crashed heavily into the side of a car, setting off its alarm.

"This is not you, Melanie!" I yelled. My K-Pistol was way out of reach, and Melanie was coming at me again.

She crushed me against the car door with her telekinesis, my head pressed up against the glass window, my limbs immobile. She was closing in, pulling back a curled fist, ready to strike.

She had to know.

"Melanie, wait!" I cried, taking a heavy breath. "It's me, Violet!"

"Violet?"

"Yes, Melanie, it's me! I'm one of the Super Secret!"

She froze, then reached over and yanked my mask right off my face.

"Violet?" she stumbled backwards, shocked. "You're Koolara?"

"Yes! I kept skipping school because I was busy protecting Diamond City as Koolara. I'm never excited to meet the Super Secret because I see them all the time, and that's how I always get the Super Show tickets!"

"But if you're Koolara... that means you knew The Shock all along..."

"Yes, but the Shock has lost his mind! We have to stop him! We have to-"

"And you never told me? You knew The Shock all along and you never told me?"

"I had to keep it a secret, I..."

She wrapped an invisible noose around my neck by simply pointing a finger. I couldn't speak, and within seconds, I was gasping for air.

And then everything turned into pitch darkness.

#13

UTMOST IMPORTANCE

I opened my eyes. Thank goodness, it was only just a dream.

My vision was blurred but was adjusting to the light. My hands felt the hard surface of the ground beneath me. My back ached. Everything hurt.

No, wait, it wasn't a dream… all that really happened. The Shock gained superpowers from the Super Diamond and had gone crazy. He wants to kill all supervillains in Diamond City. He had choked Doctor Galaxy and Electric Boy unconscious and then fought the Super Secret, his own superhero team… his own friends.

Oh, and I revealed my secret identity to Melanie, who now hates me…

"Koolara."

The Mystery was seated in front of me with his legs crossed, which was unusual for him.

"How long was I out?" I asked. "Where are we?"

My back was rested against a brick wall, and my legs were splayed like two hands of a clock. We were in an empty room that felt strangely familiar. My fingers pushed away a lock of hair that was dangling in front of my face. I wasn't wearing my mask, but that somehow didn't bother me now.

"You were unconscious for nearly two hours," The Mystery said, looking straight at me through the sharp red eyes of his mask. "We are in The Shock's building, the same one where we found you yesterday."

I looked around in surprise. Everything that used to be in here was gone, leaving the room an ugly, bare cell. The only door was to the right.

"The door is sealed shut," The Mystery said. "The walls are impenetrable. There is nothing we can do to get out. I already tried. The Shock took all our gadgets."

"Wait, what happened?" I said. "The Shock attacked you, I saw him punch you!"

The Mystery took a deep breath and laid a hand on his hip, but his utility belt wasn't there.

"My M-Belt has a healing device built into it, something similar to the M-Ring. It activated as soon as he hit me. The healing serum did not work fast enough for me to have enough strength to defend myself."

He paused.

"Lady Damage and Pandora Girl tried to stop him, but nothing could stop The Shock. The two of them and Electric Boy are held at Diamond Park, trapped there by Galaxy Ray. Doctor Galaxy is back in his cell in Diamond Prison, where the Paralysis Serum will prevent him from teleporting out. Diamond Prison and Diamond Police Force are obeying The Shock's instructions in fear that The Shock might kill them."

"Then why are we both here?" I asked, taking in all that had happened.

"Maybe The Shock still thinks that he can convince us to join his cause. He and Dream Girl threw everything out of this place. He told me about how he wants to start a brand new life as a superhero. He is currently searching for supervillains in hiding, and he is going to kill all of them, including those already in Diamond Prison. His public execution will start tomorrow in Diamond Park."

He took a deep breath, as if it had pained him physically to relate all that. "I should have kept the Super Diamond safe with me instead of leaving it in the Secret House. It was obvious that something was wrong with The Shock ever since he fought The SuperNova. He might not have shown it, but I could see that he was becoming more and more frustrated with our supervillain plague. Even after he suggested executing supervillains, I did not do anything. I could have prevented all of this. Now he has superpowers and we cannot stop him. We are all in mortal danger because of me. We have been trapped in here for an hour, and I am-"

He stared at the blank space between us. His hands were trembling.

"Koolara, I am scared."

I never thought that I would hear those words coming from the Mystery. I took a deep breath to compose myself. I was crushed by everything that had happened, but as long as The Mystery and I and the rest of the Super Secret were still alive, we could still do something to stop The Shock.

"Scared?" I said, forcing a tiny laugh. "The Mystery isn't scared of bad guys! All the supervillains of Diamond City *tremble* when they hear The Mystery is coming for them! Come on, we've been in worse situations than this. Nothing can trap The Mystery, nobody can outthink The Mystery. The Mystery is always prepared for anything. We'll find a way to get out of here and save Diamond City!"

The Mystery remained motionless, his eyes still fixed on the floor.

"We'll figure something out," I continued, my voice starting to falter. "We always do…"

It wasn't working.

"I have a way to get out of here," he said.

He shifted his body and fished out two ordinary looking black gloves from a compartment on his cape.

"Wear these," he handed them to me. "They will get you out."

"Get me out?" I took the gloves from him, confused. "What are these?"

"The M-Gloves can phase you through a solid object," he said seriously. "You can pass though the wall of this building and escape. You can save Diamond City."

My brain was trying to process everything that he was telling me. Was he really asking me to... walk through walls? With these *gloves*?

"The M-Gloves were always meant to be for myself," he continued. "It was one of the first gadgets I invented when I became The Mystery. I kept it on me at all times, so that if I were ever trapped, I could escape easily. I never had to use it in the past year. The Shock probably thought they were normal gloves and did not bother to take them from me. I was going to use them to get out of this building, but that would mean leaving you in here alone, and I cannot do that. The Shock's public execution is tomorrow, so there is no time to waste. You have to use the gloves to get out of here now."

I wanted to protest, but his sharp gaze silenced me. I gulped and relented.

I took off my own gloves and slid the M-Gloves on. There was a slight tingling sensation on my skin as I wriggled my fingers.

"Okay…" I eyed the gloves. "So how do these work?"

"Just press the button on the back of each glove, and your body's molecular formation will phase out, allowing you to pass through another solid object for three seconds. It has enough power to only be used once, but it is what you must do after you get out that is of utmost importance."

"And what would that be?" I asked, wondering if it was too late to question the science of the M-Gloves.

"You need to infiltrate Diamond Prison and disable the Paralysis Serum in Doctor Galaxy."

"Doctor Galaxy?" my eyes widened in disbelief. "Why him?"

"Doctor Galaxy can use his teleportation ability to get us to the Super Secret before The Shock notices and reacts. We need his help to rescue the others."

"But… to get help from Doctor Galaxy? Is there any other way?"

"I have thought about other solutions, but this is our best bet given the circumstances."

The gears in my brain started to spin with more and more questions, but… *The Mystery will figure it out*, Electric Boy's last words before he passed out rang in my mind. I guess I just had to trust my fellow superhero.

"Okay…" I said. "But how am I supposed to get into Diamond Prison? And how do I disable the Paralysis Serum?"

"Before I became The Mystery, I invented gadgets with someone who goes by the codename The Sleepless. Every evening, he goes to the All-Star Coffee café on the opposite side of the road from Amazing Fashion. Find him. He always wears T-shirts with rock bands on it, so he should not be too hard to identify. Tell him that The Mystery sent you and that he has to help you save Diamond City. He can give you the gadgets you need to get into Diamond Prison. The Shock may be invincible, but I have thought of a way that could at least weaken his body. I just need to invent the right gadget."

I bit my lip. "So I have to somehow convince your friend, The Sleepless, *and* our deadliest enemy, Doctor Galaxy, to help me for this plan to work. What if I can't do it? What if they don't want to help me? I mean, I'm not really the *convincing* type. What if I say something wrong and make things worse?"

The Mystery must have sensed my increasing nerves.

"Tell The Sleepless that if he helps you, you will give him the M-Gloves," he said. "He has always wanted the M-Glove's phasing technology."

"But if the two of you invented gadgets together, wouldn't he already have that technology?"

The Mystery fell silent. I realised that I might have struck a wrong nerve.

"That was a long time ago," he said. "Things have changed."

"What about Doctor Galaxy?" I felt bad and tried to change the subject. "How do I convince him to help us?"

"Saving us would mean saving himself too. He will not be killed by The Shock."

"Yeah, but he *hates* us, remember? Maybe he'd rather die than help us."

"Tell him that if he helps us, we will get Diamond Prison to release him."

"What? You can't be serious. I thought you were against

releasing supervillains early."

"I do not want to do it, but things are different now. Between releasing a supervillain and saving the lives of many, I prioritise the latter. But use this only as a last resort, only if nothing else works."

"I guess desperate times call for desperate measures," I murmured, rubbing my hands together nervously.

"Relax, Koolara," The Mystery said. "You can do it. Everything is going to be fine. The plan is going to work."

"Because you invented it," I almost laughed. He wasn't amused.

I stood up and felt a new energy rush through me. I ran the entire plan through my mind again, but there were still so many things that could go wrong…

"Koolara," The Mystery said with an unusual spark of warmth in his voice. "Thank you for believing in me."

I smiled awkwardly. "You're welcome."

"Any other questions?"

"Actually, there's something I'm dying to know," I said. "Why don't you talk with contractions?"

The Mystery cocked his head. "What do you mean?"

"Like, instead of saying, *I don't know*, you'll say *I do not know*. Or, instead of *there's no time to waste*, you'll say, *there is no time to waste*. You never talk with contractions."

The Mystery was silent for a moment, but then he flung his cape dramatically around his body. "That is my secret."

I chuckled softly, and maybe The Mystery did too... just maybe.

"There is no time to waste," The Mystery said urgently, reminding me of the situation at hand. "Remember, find The Sleepless and Doctor Galaxy. Convince them to help you save Diamond City."

I nodded and positioned myself in front of the wall next to the sealed door, gloved palms pressed against the concrete. I took one last glance at The Mystery, who gave an assuring nod, and then turned back to concentrate on passing through the wall.

I pushed the circular button on the back of each glove, and the tingling sensation on my skin increased drastically. It was like my body was being sucked into a giant vacuum cleaner. I pressed my palms against the solid wall again and felt my hands sinking in...

The Mystery said I only had three seconds. I had no time to hesitate. I squeezed my eyes shut and took the biggest step I could, almost leaping forward. In that moment, the world around me felt like it had stopped, frozen like a photograph.

The feeling passed, and suddenly, I felt normal again.

I opened my eyes. I was out of the building, standing in the middle of the forest.

Okay, Violet. Time to go home, get changed, and then find this guy called The Sleepless.

NEXT TIME

VIOLET FINDS THE SLEEPLESS!

#14

CLEAR YOUR MIND

Remember, find The Sleepless and Doctor Galaxy. Convince them to help you save Diamond City.

That was what The Mystery told me after he gave me two gloves that allowed me to pass through walls and escape the building that we were trapped in. Yeah, it sounds absolutely ridiculous, but it really happened. Apparently, the M-Gloves could only be used once, so it's not like I could run through walls now.

After heading home for a quick change into my civilian wear, I went to All-Star Coffee on Diamond Central Street to find The Mystery's friend, The Sleepless. I just hoped that he was easy to talk to.

I spotted him the moment I stepped into the famous café filled with the rich aroma of coffee. His oversized T-shirt bore the logo of Death Clock, a rock band that I've heard of but had never gotten into. His hair was a little messy, and he was pale, as if he hadn't seen the sun for weeks.

I took the seat opposite him at the corner booth and surprised him by addressing him by his codename. That name must have been a secret between only The Mystery and him.

"Who are you?" he demanded, his dark eyes boring into mine. "How did you know that name?"

"I'm Koolara," I replied, taking a chance at revealing my Super Secret identity. "The Mystery sent me."

"The Mystery?" The Sleepless raised an eyebrow sceptically, his gaze questioning. "Where is he now?"

"We were both trapped in the forest behind Diamond Park by The Shock, but The Mystery gave me the M-Gloves to escape. He's still trapped there," I related quickly in a single breath.

"Hmm," he folded his arms. "Everyone can see Electric Boy, Lady Damage and Pandora Girl trapped at Diamond Park, but we're wondering where Koolara and The Mystery are. Some even say you two deserted the Super Secret."

"We would never do that," I responded quickly, wary of the people seated in the booths near us. Best to keep this short and sweet. "The Shock brought the two of us to a different location because he wanted to talk to us separately... but that's beside the point. Mystery sent me here to find you because we need your help."

"The Mystery wants *my* help?" he almost sneered.

"He said he invented gadgets with you, and you could give

me the gadgets I need."

"Yes, we worked on gadgets together some time ago, but didn't he tell you?" The Sleepless leaned back in his seat. "He deserted me."

Just as I suspected, it sounded like there had been some unpleasant history between the two. The mission of convincing The Sleepless to help me had just become that much harder.

"We need your help to protect Diamond City from The Shock," I appealed. "We have to stop him."

"Hey, The Shock's just doing what he thinks is best for Diamond City."

"He's going to *kill* people."

"He's going to kill *supervillains*... bad people!"

"They're already serving their time in Diamond Prison according to their crimes. That's what the law is for. The Shock doesn't have the right to kill anybody on his own accord. Even supervillains should be given the chance to change for the better."

"Even Doctor Galaxy?"

"Yes, even Doctor Galaxy," I said, remembering the look on Doctor Galaxy's face as he was being choked unconscious by The Shock. I remembered his pleading look when he wordlessly begged for us to save him... which we didn't.

"Ah, I'm just messing with you," The Sleepless said airily, suddenly dropping his guarded manner. "Even *I* can't justify killing. The Shock must be out of his super-mind. Sure, I'll help you this time, but…" He drummed his fingers on the table. "What's in it for me?"

Just as expected, he wanted something in return. I guessed that now was as good a time as any to use my blue chip, so I fished out the two M-Gloves from my pocket and laid them on the table. "If you help me, you can have these."

The Sleepless' eyes lit up instantly. He picked up the M-Gloves carefully and examined them for a full minute before he smiled, satisfied with my proposal. He put the gloves back on the table between us.

"It's a deal," he said. "So, what gadgets do you want from me?"

"I need gadgets which can help me infiltrate Diamond Prison," I said. "I need to get in undetected and disable the Paralysis Serum that prevents Doctor Galaxy from teleporting out. The Mystery's plan is to use Doctor Galaxy's teleportation ability to rescue the rest of the Super Secret and take down The Shock together."

The Sleepless clasped his hands together, and I waited for a response.

"I can put a bunch of stuff together," he finally said. "It's best to go at midnight. You'll need night vision goggles to see in the dark, micro-electrical pulse disruptors to shut off the motion sensor alarms and laser security system, a far-range wireless data scrambler to hack the security camera feed..."

He listed several other equipment, and I nodded accordingly, trying to absorb as much information as I could. I wasn't sure if he was done, but he paused when a waitress with long flowy hair and pointed lashes came up to our table.

"Would you like a refill, Mr White?" she asked.

"No, thank you," The Sleepless glanced at her, seemingly irritated that his real last name had been revealed. The waitress nodded and walked away.

"Come here often?" I asked.

"Yes," he inhaled. "I spend all my time at home working on my gadgets, but I come here when I want to relax. It's a good place to have a coffee and clear your mind."

He was right. This was a pretty great place to sit down, have a drink and simply relax. I must have walked past this café a million times but had never once thought of coming in. Not without Melanie, at least.

"So, what happened between you and The Mystery?" I

asked, my curiosity getting the better of me. "You said he deserted you?"

"Yes," his face turned sour. "He can be really selfish and cold towards other people, even his friends... if he even *has* any left."

"The Mystery I know isn't cold and selfish," I retorted. "In fact, he's one of the most caring and selfless people I know."

"Maybe you just haven't known him long enough."

"The Mystery can be..." I searched for the right words. "Overly serious, but he isn't cold and selfish."

"Maybe you should ask him what happened... what he did to me."

As much as I was curious, I had to focus on the present mission. Time *was* of the essence.

"I'll ask him if it comes up," I said. "So, where are all those gadgets I need?"

"Get yourself a coffee. I'll be back in an hour."

NEXT TIME

KOOLARA TALKS TO DOCTOR GALAXY AGAIN!

#15

TWO PERSON THING

The Sleepless' gadgets were fortunately lightweight and easy to strap onto my utility belt and thigh holster. A flood of nervousness washed over me as I approached Diamond Prison. It was close to midnight, and I had to get going if I were to complete the mission.

The night vision goggles helped me to navigate in the dark as I successfully disabled the security fences around Diamond Prison, which I then climbed over stealthily. A password hacking device, similar to the M-Matcher, was used to gain access to the Supervillain Building.

The micro-electrical pulse disruptors rendered the laser security system useless, and the far-range wireless data scrambler tapped into all the cameras that guarded the corridors, freezing all footage of the empty corridors so that they wouldn't pick me up. There were guards on patrol at midnight, but I slipped past all of them. I heaved a sigh of relief when I reached Doctor Galaxy's cell unscathed and undetected, but the mission was far from over.

The lights flicked on automatically as the heavy door slid

open with a whoosh, the harsh lighting making me squint. I stepped into the prison cell which contained a single bed, a stack of paperback novels and nothing else. The four walls were a plain metallic white, and the air was as cold as the dark night outside. I pulled the door close behind me, and it locked with a click.

Doctor Galaxy was lying in bed with his head on a pillow. He stared at me silently from where he was without stirring, unperturbed by my sudden entrance.

"Doctor Galaxy," I addressed him, my voice filling the emptiness around me a little louder than I expected. "This is going to be hard to believe… but I need you to help the Super Secret."

Doctor Galaxy eyed me mutinously, and then, as if he hadn't heard, turned away with his back to me, apparently trying to get back to sleep. How could he even sleep when he might die tomorrow?

"I said, I need you to help the Super Secret," I repeated forcefully. "The Shock is looking for all supervillains in hiding and plans to kill all of them. You need to help us stop him."

"Help the Super Secret?" he finally spoke as he turned back to me. "Why would I want to help any of you?"

"You're going to *die* tomorrow if you don't. If you help us, we can stop The Shock, and you'll survive."

"The Shock is invincible. You saw it with your own eyes. Nothing can hurt him. Besides, he injected me with the Paralysis Serum. I can't leave Diamond Prison. You, of all people, should know that."

"Listen to me. I can disable the Paralysis Serum. Once I do that, you'll be able to teleport us to Diamond Park, where the Super Secret are trapped, and rescue them. Together, we can take down The Shock."

Doctor Galaxy gave a sardonic chuckle. "Sounds like a plan... but I wouldn't want to help the Super Secret, even if it means being publicly executed."

My fears of hitting a brick wall were confirmed, but I sensed a hint of pain and regret in Doctor Galaxy's voice.

"Why?" I asked. "Why do you hate the Super Secret so much? I mean, other supervillains want to rob banks or take over the city, but you only seem to want to hurt us."

He remained still, but then he slowly sat up straight, shifting himself to the edge of the bed and setting his feet on the ground. He combed his black hair over the back of his head with one hand and massaged his neck. He looked like he wanted to speak, but still he hesitated.

"Come on, you can tell me," I assured, walking over to the bed. The mattress bounced a little as I sat next to him. Being this close certainly put me in the most vulnerable position, but I wasn't afraid. I needed to show him that he could trust me.

"I promise it'll stay between us," I added.

He sighed, and I suddenly realised how young he was. He couldn't have been much older than me, but his cool green eyes bore a regretful sorrow. My impression of him was shaped by the media, but now that I'm seated beside him, I realised that "Diamond City's deadliest supervillain" might be more of a misunderstood one.

"I know a girl... Samantha Stewart," he said. "I met her in Secondary School. Every time I look at her, I would feel a warm sensation in my chest. She's kind, gentle and never has any bad intentions towards anyone. I love her shy smile and her cute freckles. She's the loveliest girl I've ever known. We used to hang out at the mall every Sunday afternoon, and I always saw her home. Every moment I spend with her is pure magic, something I wish I can experience over and over again."

He paused to take a deep breath.

"But one Saturday, she didn't respond to my usual texts," he continued. "I even tried to call her but was still unable to reach her. I only got a reply the next day, but it was from her mum. Samantha had been admitted to the hospital. Her right leg had been broken in several places. She was in the food court when the Super

Secret was fighting Jet Coaster, and something fell on her..."

I gasped quietly. I certainly don't remember any girl getting her leg broken during a fight, which made me sad and angry at the same time.

"That made me *hate* the Super Secret," he said bitterly, his voice taut. "The media only focuses on the good parts of your battles, the parts that make people clap and cheer. The ugly side of things always gets ignored. I wanted to avenge her, so I formed a new identity as Doctor Galaxy. I had created a synthetically enhanced adhesive substance for an annual science fair, something so strong that it could actually immobilise a person. I called it *Galaxy Ray*, and I invented *Galaxy Cannons* to shoot it from my arms. I went out to Diamond City Port as Doctor Galaxy, using a show of Galaxy Ray to cause chaos and attract the Super Secret into a fight that I was absolutely confident I would win..."

He sighed, an unexpected gesture from Diamond City's deadliest supervillain.

"You know what happened next... you superheroes defeated me, and I was thrown into Diamond Prison with a sentence of two years. When The Shock came to visit me yesterday, he told me that he wanted superpowers so he could fight and *kill* supervillains easily, and he would release me from prison if I told him the secret of gaining superpowers. I could finally get out of this place, so of course I agreed. The Shock told the prison guards to administer the antidote for the Paralysis Serum so he could take me to the Secret House for some tests. Once we were out, I told him how to get superpowers from the Super Diamond…"

"The Shock said that you just needed to *touch* it long enough to get superpowers," I interjected, recalling how he had boasted about it during the fight.

"Yeah, that's the big secret," Doctor Galaxy replied in a deflated voice. "You hold it in your bare hands for about an hour, and it will give you superpowers."

The room suddenly grew colder. I waited for an elaboration, but that was it.

"I don't know how it works exactly," he sensed my confusion. "But it certainly changes something inside you. The tricky part is figuring out what superpower you actually gained. Some people like The SuperNova and the Triple Dangers discovered theirs pretty easily, but others needed a bit more time."

"How did you figure *yours* out?" I was still sceptical. "And where did you get the Super Diamond from in the first place?"

"Somebody appeared in my cell and gave it to me… I don't know who it was," Doctor Galaxy ran his fingers through his smooth hair again. "I know it sounds like I'm joking, but it's the truth. I woke up in the middle of the night when I sensed movement in my cell. A shadowy figure was standing beside my bed, and he put this glowing purple diamond right beside me. Before I could see his face, he vanished as suddenly as he appeared. I touched the diamond, just to feel if it was real, and even though I could hold it, I thought that it was all just a weird dream, and went back to sleep. I was shocked when I discovered that the diamond was still in my hand when I woke up in the morning. I even suspected that one of the prison guards might be playing a prank on me..."

He glanced at me to check if I was still listening, and I was, so he continued his story.

"That morning, I was the first one in the bathroom as per usual. I was just thinking about going back to my cell to do some reading before breakfast. Suddenly, I was standing on this very bed. I couldn't believe it. So I tried an experiment and concentrated on returning to where I was a second ago. The next thing I knew, I found myself in the bathroom again, staring at my own reflection in the mirror. I put two and two together and realised that this had something to do with the diamond. Somehow, it must have given me teleportation abilities, which I spent the next few days practicing. I got the hang of my new superpower eventually."

"And all this happened... when?"

"About two weeks before The SuperNova appeared in

Amazing Fashion with superpowers. I'd passed the Super Diamond to Mr Magic when he visited me in prison, and the guards never questioned anything. He was passing me Space Savers novels every month anyway. I told Mr Magic about what happened to me and what this diamond could do. Our plan was to form a superpowered team that would free me from prison. We would defeat the Super Secret once and for all and take whatever we wanted from Diamond City. Unfortunately, that plan didn't happen, because everyone who got superpowers only cared about themselves and used their superpowers to fulfil their own selfish goals."

He paused in dismay. "Even if I escaped prison now, I can't visit her in hospital... because she knows I'm Doctor Galaxy."

He was talking about Samantha, the girl he was in love with. So avenging her was the reason he became Doctor Galaxy in the first place.

"I'm sorry," I said at last. "I'm sorry she got injured so badly because of one of our fights. We didn't mean to cause casualties. The whole point of us putting our lives on the line is to protect the people of Diamond City from danger."

He didn't say anything. He just stared at the empty floor in front of him.

"The Shock wants to protect innocent people from getting hurt," I continued. "He wants it so bad that he's willing to kill supervillains to achieve his goal. But it's wrong of him to take the law into his own hands. He has no right to kill anybody, even if they're guilty. You want to stop innocent people from getting hurt too, but fighting the Super Secret is not the answer. You can do it the right way now if you help us take down The Shock. It's the only way to stop more people from getting hurt, or killed."

Still nothing.

"Here," I detached a gadget from my utility belt. It looked like a pen with a transparent slit on its side and a single button at its end. The Sleepless called it a *Chemical Manipulator.*

"This is already programmed to remove the Paralysis Serum inside your body completely," I said. "You just have to be within five feet of this device when it's switched on."

"How long will it take?"

"About six hours, but it'll remove the serum entirely, and you'll be able to teleport out of Diamond Prison and get us to the rest of the Super Secret. So, will you help me?" I held up the pen. "If I remove the serum?"

"I'll help you with your little plan... if you remove the serum *and* tell Diamond Prison to officially release me, so I don't become an escaped prisoner."

I gulped. Just like The Mystery said, all he wanted was to be a free man, but then again, which prisoner didn't? I glanced down at the gadget in my hand. I had no other choice. I had to make a deal in order to get Doctor Galaxy's help, so I nodded and pushed the button. The transparent slit on the side beamed in bright green, signalling that it was active.

"Great," Doctor Galaxy sounded satisfied, kicking back to lie down on the mattress, hands behind his head. My fists clenched instinctively for a second, ready to defend myself from a surprise attack, but Doctor Galaxy didn't move. The tension in the room seemed to have lifted a little, but it didn't make the situation any less serious.

"Don't be so uptight, Koolara," he glanced at me. "You have a pen that negates the best security technology in Diamond City. Sure, it takes hours, but you should be fascinated. How does The Mystery invent all these gadgets anyway? Does he have a whole team of scientists working for him or something?"

"Umm, no," I said, surprised by Doctor Galaxy's sudden change in spirit. It reminded me of talking to the boys in Secondary School. "And this isn't The Mystery's."

"Then where did it come from?"

"A friend."

"Seems like there're more than a few geniuses in Diamond

City… and all I could invent was super sticky *glue*."

He pulled a face, and I couldn't help but chuckle.

"You're not going to just sit on my bed and stare at your feet till morning, are you?" Doctor Galaxy said.

"Of course not," I got up and settled in a corner of the cell. "You can go back to sleep if you want."

"I'm going to be out of here in six hours. I'm too hyped up to go back to sleep now."

He reached out to grab one of the books from the pile on his bed, holding it up for me to see. The cover was a dazzling outer space landscape with a futuristic space vehicle speeding towards the fourth wall.

"*Space Savers: Trouble on Spaceworld*," he read the title out loud. "It's an all-new story based on the original Space Savers TV show."

"Hmm," I made a noise.

"Do you want to read it?" he asked.

I didn't know how to respond to his strange request.

"We're stuck in here for six hours anyway," he added. "Oh, I get it. You're not into Space Savers."

"I *love* Space Savers. It's one of my favourite TV shows."

"Great, then we can read this book together!" His face had lit up, friendly and eager.

Did he actually say that we could read this book together? I loved reading a good science fiction novel, but now? In prison? With a supervillain? The logical part of my brain was shouting at me to reject his ridiculous offer, but what harm could reading a book possibly bring? It would definitely help to pass time…

"But…" I said. "You can't read a book together with someone. It's not like a movie. Reading is more of a *one* person thing."

"It can be a *two* person thing," he moved to the other side of the bed, where it met the wall and gestured to the space on the mattress.

I wasn't quite sure what he meant, but I decided to play along, reminding myself that staying awake and alert was better than accidentally falling asleep. I kept my eyes on him as I went over to the bed again. I rested my back against the cold metallic wall and straightened my legs out on the soft mattress.

"We can read at the same time," he held the book in front of us and opened it to the first page. "Once you've read the last word of the page, just give the thumbs up, and I'll turn to the next page."

"What if you haven't read to the end of the page?" I asked.

"Relax, Koolara. I've already read this book."

"Then should we read another one?"

"I like this one. I want to read it again."

And so we began our weird reading session together.

The first few pages went by fairly slowly, mostly because I delayed my thumbs up to make sure that he had also completed the current page. I wasn't too sure if he was really reading along because I caught him glancing at me a couple of times. I would pretend not to notice, but I caught him staring once, and he immediately reverted his gaze back to the book.

As our reading went on, I began to relax and give my thumbs up sooner. I laughed at the funny bits, and he laughed along with me, occasionally throwing in some trivia from the TV show that we both loved.

Spaceworld was an intergalactic holiday resort on a small isolated planet for anyone who wanted a fun and relaxing time away from their home world. The President of Spaceworld contacted the Space Savers for help because there was a terrible crisis in the city. People were developing strange marks on their bodies, and whoever had these marks wouldn't survive past another day. Many scrambled to return to their home planets, but a massive space storm prevented the shuttles from departing safely. The Space Savers were on the case, but they would soon discover, to their horror, that Spaceworld was much more than it seemed…

The story was so gripping that even though I felt the lull of sleep, the secret behind Spaceworld kept me wide awake. The only thing I wanted now was to know what Spaceworld really was! Doctor Galaxy said I would never guess how the story ends. I threw out a few theories, but he wouldn't tell me if they were right or wrong.

"No spoilers," he teased.

We finished the entire book in under four hours.

"Wow," I said. "That ending totally blew my mind."

"Yeah," he yawned. "Told you you'll never guess what happens at the end."

"The Red Saver is my favourite," I said. "He just seems very decisive, you know. He's the guy who goes out and gets the job done."

"Yeah," he said. "The Red Saver is my favourite too. I like his outfit from the first season of the original TV show."

"*Doctor Galaxy,*" I said in sudden realisation. "You named yourself after Doctor Dream and Galaxy Racer from Space Savers!"

"Yeah," he said. "Stupid, isn't it."

"I think it's cool."

"Why did you call yourself Koolara?"

I blinked. I've been asked that so many times, but I've never given a straight answer before, mainly because the real answer was too ridiculous and embarrassing.

"It's okay if you don't want to tell me."

"Nah, it's fine," I said. "I just assumed the reason was pretty obvious."

"Obvious?" he repeated blankly. So I told him, and he burst out in laughter, clutching his stomach with both hands. "That *can't* be true..."

"It is," I said. "Come on, it's not that funny."

"It's just... so random," he looked at me with a goofy grin on his face.

"It's better than *Super Diamond*," I said. "You made up that name, didn't you?"

"It's a diamond that gives superpowers, what else was I going to call it?"

"Ha," I snorted, suppressing a yawn with one hand. I wondered if getting too comfortable with a supervillain was a mistake, but there was no harm in a little chit chat, was there?

"Does your family visit you here often?" I asked.

"I have no family," he replied nonchalantly. "They passed away when I was still a baby... are you close to your parents?"

"I guess so... while they were still alive."

We didn't speak for a while, but it wasn't an uncomfortable silence. I thought about my parents, my childhood. I caught him glancing at me from the corner of his eye again.

"What happened?" he asked.

"They were murdered last year," I said. "The police never caught the murderer."

"Oh... I'm sorry. I'm sure your parents were nice people."

"They were the best. I wish I could bring them back."

"At least you got to spend time with them."

"I'm sure your parents were nice people too."

"Maybe... but they'll be pretty disappointed if they saw me now. Their son is Diamond City's deadliest supervillain and a celebrity prisoner."

"You don't have to be Doctor Galaxy anymore."

"We can teleport to Diamond Park in the morning," he said, ignoring my comment. "The Paralysis Serum should be completely removed by then."

"Yeah..." I said in the middle of another big yawn.

Doctor Galaxy got off the bed and went to the other side of the cell, lying flat on the cold, hard ground. He was holding the Chemical Manipulator in one hand, and somehow, I wasn't worried.

"You can sleep on the bed if you want," he said. "I'll be fine right here."

I nodded, but I didn't move from my spot. I didn't sleep either.

We remained where we were for the next two hours, not talking but still staring at each other's general direction. I thought about everything that had happened and how it might all be over in just a few hours, *if* the plan worked. I hoped that The Mystery was alright, that The Shock hadn't returned unannounced and discover that I was gone. My mind drifted to Electric Boy, Lady Damage and Pandora Girl...

And Melanie.

When it was time, the Chemical Manipulator beeped and its light switched off, indicating that all the Paralysis Serum in its range had been eliminated.

"Koolara," Doctor Galaxy said, noticing it too. "It's time."

He walked towards me, and I stood up as well.

"You ready to go?" he asked, the green smoke circling from his feet.

I nodded, and he grabbed my hand.

The Mystery: "Koolara, are you okay?"

Koolara: "Yes, I'm okay! I did what you told me to. Did The Shock come back here?"

The Mystery: "No, but there is no time to waste. We have to go rescue the others."

Doctor Galaxy: "So, The Mystery needs *my* help, eh?"

Koolara: "No time for banter! We need to work together to save Diamond City. People's lives are at stake!"

Doctor Galaxy: "Relax, Koolara, you know I'm on your side. I'm just breaking the ice with The Mystery here... but will the rest of your super friends trust me?"

The Mystery: "When they see us with you, they will know that they can trust you."

Doctor Galaxy: "I *hope* so."

The Mystery: "Koolara, did The Sleepless give you a wireless data scrambler?"

Koolara: "Yeah, here you go..."

The Mystery: "Good. And he gave you a Chemical Manipulator too?"

Koolara: "Yeah, he programmed an additional setting that can neutralise Galaxy Ray. We can free the others once we get there."

The Mystery: "Okay, then we stick to the plan. Take us to Diamond Park, to the outdoor concert stage where the Secret Show takes place. That is where the others are held at."

Doctor Galaxy: "Let's go, then. Let's get this over and done with."

Pandora Girl: "Look, it's Koolara! And The Mystery!"

Electric Boy: "Watch out, Doctor Galaxy is behind you!"

Koolara: "Relax, guys, he's with us."

Lady Damage: "What do you mean, he's with us? How did you two escape from The Shock?"

Koolara: "It's complicated, I'll explain later… look, I can free you guys with *this*!"

Electric Boy: "Am I the only one who remembers that Doctor Galaxy is a *supervillain*?"

The Mystery: "Doctor Galaxy rescued me and Koolara. We can trust him. To take down The Shock, we need Doctor Galaxy's help."

Lady Damage: "What if he turns on us?"

Koolara: "It's the best option we have now. I trust him, and you can trust *me*."

Pandora Girl: "If Koolara says we can trust him, then I trust him."

Lady Damage: "Okay, fine… but get me out of this quick!"

Electric Boy: "I didn't get any sleep last night…"

The Mystery: "If my calculations are correct, the Galaxy Ray should lose its adhesive properties in three minutes."

Lady Damage: "Then let's hope The Shock or his girlfriend doesn't come back here in that time. A few police squads tried rescuing us, but Dream Girl fought them all off. She's stopping anyone who tries to come into Diamond Park."

Electric Boy: "I wonder what The Shock is doing out there. He hasn't returned since he left us here."

Pandora Girl: "I feel the Galaxy Ray getting softer."

The Mystery: "I have a way to take down The Shock. Here is the plan…"

#16

STOP FIGHTING

We were in the outdoor stage area of Diamond Park where our Secret Shows were usually held, only today, the event here couldn't be more different and dangerous. I had switched the Chemical Manipulator to its second setting and used it to negate the adhesive properties of the Galaxy Ray, freeing Electric Boy, Lady Damage and Pandora Girl within a span of mere minutes. They had been cautiously eyeing Doctor Galaxy, who was still decked in his strikingly bright orange prison uniform and was looking decidedly uncomfortable.

"The Chemical Manipulator," The Mystery said as soon as our friends were freed.

I handed the gadget to The Mystery, who went to work on it immediately, plying open the bottom of the pen and connecting a cable to the wireless data scrambler, which he had been relentlessly fiddling with ever since we grabbed him out of The Shock's hidden building.

"Is this going to work?" Electric Boy asked worriedly as The Mystery continued his hurried assembly of the gadgets.

"Yes," The Mystery replied simply. There had been no time for any kind of elaborate preparation, but The Mystery had cooked up something with The Sleepless' gadgets that I'd brought him, and hopefully, it would be able to weaken The Shock.

"They're here!" Pandora Girl exclaimed. She pointed behind me worriedly, and I whipped around to see The Shock and Dream Girl coming towards us from a distance.

"This is it," The Mystery said. "Everyone hang on."

The Shock stopped a short distance away from us, a mix of surprise and amusement etched on his face. Something was different with his costume. He wasn't wearing his S-Braces. I guess he didn't need them now that his entire body was invincible. Dream Girl stood beside him in her Shock hoodie, looking colder than the iciest winter. She was The Shock's sidekick now, so I guess her dream finally came true.

"In just one night, I rounded up *ten* supervillains and put them in Diamond Prison," The Shock said, lifting his chin proudly. "They will all be publicly executed, one by one, but since the Super Secret is already here, why don't we start with yours now?"

"It is not your right to kill, Shock," The Mystery urged, still trying to reason with him.

The Shock threw his head back to laugh. "Do it, my love. Show them what *real* superpowers can do!"

The girl in the Shock hoodie lifted her hand towards us, commanding an invisible force which threw The Mystery forward through the air and dropped him at her feet. As if he was controlled by strings, The Mystery rose up to a standing position, hands stuck by his side, unable to break free.

"Melanie, snap out of it!" I cried from where I was. "Think about what you're doing! Listen to me, Melanie! I'm your best friend!"

"I brought you to my hidden building to give you one last chance to join me," The Shock said as he stepped closer to The Mystery. "But you didn't appreciate my kindness. You will be the first to die."

"Do it then," The Mystery remained motionless. "No more suspense."

"As you wish," The Shock hissed.

He reached out for The Mystery's throat, but The Mystery was no longer there. In a split second, he was standing beside me, shrouded in a faint cloud of green smoke. Doctor Galaxy had teleported him back to safety in the blink of an eye, but I couldn't see Doctor Galaxy amongst the group. That meant that he had already-

"Grab them all, my-" The Shock paused abruptly when he realised that Dream Girl was no longer beside him. "What-" he jerked his head around in confusion. "What happened?"

"Do not worry, she is somewhere safe," The Mystery said. "Doctor Galaxy will make sure of that."

The Shock clenched his fists in anger. "So, what's the plan now, Mystery? I'm still invincible, and you guys don't even have your gadgets. You can't stop me!"

The Mystery held up his newly created device which had a few loose circuits hanging out from the sides.

"The tracking serum from my M-Pill is still inside you, and it can be wirelessly manipulated to produce similar effects to that of the Paralysis Serum," The Mystery explained. "I can do it all from this modified chemical scrambler in my hand. Once the conversion of the serum is completed, you will be severely weakened. You will not be invincible anymore."

"You *can't* do that," The Shock chuckled. "Convert the serum in my body? That's impossible!"

"It is possible," The Mystery said. "I invented it."

The Shock narrowed his eyes. "You're lying."

"I activated the conversion as soon as you came within range," The Mystery tapped the screen of the device. "And it will be completed by the time I finish this sentence."

"You can't defeat me-" The Shock suddenly groaned on

cue, clutching his heart as the serum came into effect. "I-I'm invincible…"

We watched with bated breath as the pain passed him. He recovered slightly, clenching and unclenching his fists, but something must have felt different to him, because The Shock's expression changed into one of realisation and then rage. The Mystery's plan must have worked. The serum had weakened him.

"I don't need to be invincible to defeat you all," The Shock glared at us and began to advance recklessly, seething with angry determination to take us all down.

"Get ready!" Lady Damage shifted into her combat stance.

"He is severely weakened but still stronger than the average human being," The Mystery glanced at the readings on his gadget before pocketing it away. "We can take him down together, but everyone be extra careful."

"Will do, Mystery!" Electric Boy was bouncing on the balls of his feet like a ready-coiled spring.

He was the first to charge towards The Shock, who held his ground despite the effects of the serum. Electric Boy swung his fists while The Shock defended each blow evenly. They were well-matched until The Shock caught Electric Boy off-guard with a feint. Electric Boy didn't react fast enough and received a direct blow in the face. He tripped backwards and crashed heavily to the ground.

Lady Damage signalled to me and Pandora Girl, and we surrounded The Shock. She dashed forward quickly and leapt into the air, aiming her foot at The Shock's face. The Shock shifted to the side to dodge the kick, and then he grabbed her by the ankle and swung her away.

I lashed out at The Shock with my bare hands, but I had sparred with him long enough such that he anticipated every punch that I threw him. He smirked as he jabbed, the blows much heavier than when we practiced. I could barely keep up trying to block him, and there was almost no time to recover to counter him.

I heard a wild yell before I saw Pandora Girl leap onto The Shock from behind and strangled him with a choke-hold, her arm fastened around his neck. She jerked, and The Shock pulled away from me for a much needed couple of seconds, but he grabbed her quickly by the arm and flung her recklessly at me. We crashed to the ground, my back bearing the brunt of the impact against the pavement.

The Mystery attacked wordlessly before The Shock could recover. What The Mystery lacked in strength, he made up for in speed. His punches were swift and sure, and his rhythm was throwing The Shock off.

The Mystery had delivered a firm strike to The Shock's

throat and followed with a barrage of blows to his head, finally knocking The Shock to the ground. It looked as though The Mystery had won, but The Shock made a mad swipe at The Mystery's legs, and The Mystery fell hard.

The Shock took his chance, grabbing The Mystery and slamming him into a lamp post, a ghastly ring echoing from where The Mystery met metal. The Mystery cried out and crumpled to the ground. He was no match for The Shock's strength.

The Shock straightened, cracking his knuckles and wiping the blood from the corner of his mouth with the back of his hand.

"Time to die," he grinned manically, taking a step towards The Mystery.

He didn't see Doctor Galaxy materialise behind him, a plank of wood in his grasp. Doctor Galaxy smashed his weapon hard on The Shock's back, the wood cracking and splintering with the force. The Shock shuddered and involuntarily dropped onto his knees. Doctor Galaxy swung the plank of wood a second time from the side like a baseball bat, this time catching The Shock on the shoulder. The Shock lifted his arms instinctively to defend himself, but without his S-Braces, his right arm absorbed the full impact of the next swing. The Shock cried and hunkered down as the weapon met its mark.

I watched them, my heart pounding loudly in my ears. The

scene seemed too familiar. Just yesterday, the roles had been reversed. It had been The Shock who had threatened Doctor Galaxy, and we didn't do anything to protect him.

I won't make the same mistake twice. I won't just stand here and do nothing as people get hurt, not if I can do something about it. I chose to be a superhero, and a superhero *protects* people.

As Doctor Galaxy raised the plank of wood again, I ran between the two and pushed them apart.

"Stop it!" I screamed, shielding The Shock from Doctor Galaxy. "Stop fighting!"

Doctor Galaxy glared at me.

"Move aside, Koolara," he growled. "I can beat him."

"Violence is not the answer!"

"He was going to kill all of us!" Doctor Galaxy retorted, still holding his primitive weapon.

"So were you!" I glared pointedly. "Just because he tried to kill us doesn't mean you have the right to kill him too!"

I turned to The Shock, who was drawing in deep breaths, staggering as he glared at Doctor Galaxy. "Please… I know you, Shock," I pleaded. "I know that deep down inside, all you want to do is protect people and protect this city. But taking the law into our own hands is not what superheroes do. It's not *right*, Shock."

"Even if the supervillains don't learn their lesson in prison? Even if they come out to harm innocent people again?" The Shock winced in pain as he glanced at Doctor Galaxy. "Does *he* deserve another chance?"

"Yes. I gave it to him, and he used it well," I responded. "And now, I'm giving one to *you* as well, even after what *you've* done."

The Shock stumbled to his feet, breathing heavily and clutching his injured shoulder. "All I've done is protect Diamond City."

"All you've done is terrorise Diamond City," I said. "You can't protect Diamond City by killing supervillains. That justice is not for us to execute. Look at the people around you..."

The Shock looked around him, suddenly aware of the crowd of people who had gathered around the scene and were watching fearfully from a safe enough distance. News crews with their big cameras had arrived. There were policemen aiming their guns, but they didn't come near. Many were pointing at us, whispering and murmuring, whipping out their phones to take photos.

We caught snatches of "The Shock" and "supervillain", and I saw a look of horror cross The Shock's face. The Shock, beloved superhero of Diamond City, was now being labelled as the newest supervillain. He had become his own worst fear. The people didn't think that he was protecting them. To them, he was wrecking the city.

The Shock, stunned by the revelation, swallowed twice before he found his voice. "I didn't know they were frightened of me... are they frightened of me?"

"These are the people you promised to protect," I continued. "So protect them. Whether or not the law condemns criminals to die or to be put in prison is out of our hands, but we can still do what we can as superheroes. Round up criminals and let them be judged under the law, just like what we've been doing for the past year. Be a *real* superhero. Be the superhero who inspired *me* to become one too."

The Shock lowered his head, trying to hide his face. Behind me, Doctor Galaxy dropped his weapon.

I heard movement and realised that the police were closing in.

"Put your hands where I can see them, Shock!" the Commissioner of Police stammered into the megaphone as they advanced, obviously not thrilled that they were facing The Shock. The Shock complied and didn't resist when they cuffed him.

"We'll take it from here," the Commissioner said, signalling to his team. "But I think we'll need Paralysis Serum for this guy."

"And me," Doctor Galaxy added surprisingly, offering his wrists for the cuffs. "I need to serve the rest of my sentence."

I turned to him. "I thought we had a deal. I mean to keep my word, you know, about that early release."

He shrugged. "I changed my mind."

I smiled. "Thank you for helping."

"It was my pleasure, Koolara," he replied, before being escorted away by the police.

The Mystery limped over to where The Shock was being taken away.

"Shock," he called out. "We will welcome you back, if you so wish after your sentence."

The Shock turned to look at us, his shoulders hunched.

"Mystery, Koolara, everybody... I'm sorry," The Shock said brokenly. "I really am."

He ducked into the police car without waiting for our reply, and we watched in silence as it pulled away.

"Are you okay?" Lady Damage came up beside me with Electric Boy and Pandora Girl in tow.

"Yeah," I couldn't help sighing as I watched the car disappearing down the road.

"Relax, Koolara," The Mystery placed his hand on my shoulder. "Everything is going to be okay."

#17

CONTINUE TO BE SUPERHEROES

"Here it comes!" Electric Boy exclaimed.

We were gathered in the Secret House and watching the local evening news from the big monitor in the main meeting room, waiting for the exclusive interview which we knew was coming. The giant headline onscreen screamed *"EXCLUSIVE INTERVIEW WITH KOOLARA!"*

It was three days after what the media had dubbed as the "Evil Shock" incident, and that was all that everyone in Diamond City could talk about. The titles faded to a news anchor with curly blonde hair and perfectly straight white teeth standing in Diamond Park. This interview was taped just this morning.

"That's right, people of Diamond City, we have an exclusive interview with the superhero on everyone's lips, the main star herself, Koolara!" she was saying into the camera as the screen panned to include me in the frame.

"So Koolara, *what happened* to The Shock?" the news anchor prompted in her overly enthusiastic voice. "What made him decide to go on a supervillain killing spree, and how did you change his mind?"

"All The Shock wanted to do was to protect Diamond City," I heard myself saying and cringed inwardly at my voice. "But he didn't go about it the right way. He understands that now and will reflect on that in Diamond Prison."

"What will happen to the Super Secret without The Shock? Will Diamond City still have her teenage crime-fighting superhero team?"

"We will still be here to protect Diamond City. The Super Secret will continue to be superheroes."

"Well, that's a relief!"

"I just want to say something…" I stuttered, and the camera panned such that I seemed to be directly addressing the viewers. "Even though the Super Secret always tries to take down criminals and supervillains in the most efficient and safest ways possible, we are aware that our fights may still result in casualties and damage of public property. We would like to apologise for that."

The interview cut to scenes of people taking pictures of us and re-enactments from excited witnesses. Footage of the Super Secret's hospital visits over the past three days rolled one after the other.

"You nailed that interview, Koolara," Electric Boy

remarked.

"I never knew Koolara was such a good speaker," Lady Damage chimed in, giving me the thumbs up and a wink.

"It was a really good idea for us to visit the hospitals," Pandora Girl said. The team had gone at my suggestion, and all the patients had been thrilled to see us, much to our delight. We even handed out Super Secret Stuff for free.

The Mystery patted my shoulder, which stunned everyone. He wasn't known for gestures of the sort.

"Thanks guys," I felt myself turning red. I was not used to being the centre of attention, even in the team.

It should have ended on a celebratory note for us, except that the news report cut to include The Shock's sentence as well. Despite our best attempts at protecting The Shock's reputation, the incriminating footage of The Shock fighting us and his misdeeds had earned him three years in Diamond Prison. That's even longer than Doctor Galaxy's sentence.

Nobody said anything immediately, and the mood in the Secret House had gone unusually sombre and quiet. The news cut to a cheesy advertisement on the newly released Super Secret Stuff, and The Mystery switched it off.

Thankfully, Melanie's identity had been kept confidential

from the air. She had been sent to a girls' home for six months, and her parents were devastated when they received the news.

I had visited Melanie at the girls' home, but she had looked neither happy nor sad to see me. Her usual bright and bouncy demeanour was now colourless and stale, and even the soft curls in her hair looked dead. Our conversation wasn't easy.

"Melanie, I'm so sorry. I know it's too late, but I'm sorry I didn't tell you I was Koolara," I said. "You're the best friend I could ever have... I wish I could have told you. Please believe me."

She had looked past me, and I thought that she hadn't heard me, but then she whispered. "He really likes you, you know. He never got over you, even when he was with me."

"You mean... The Shock? How do you know?"

"You're all he talks about."

"*Three years?*" Electric Boy repeated in disbelief, bringing me back to the present.

"He held us against our will," Lady Damage said. "The judge actually gave him a fairly light sentence for his crimes."

"Can't we do something for The Shock?" Pandora Girl asked in a small voice. "Can we appeal the sentence?"

"Diamond City has one of the strictest laws in the world,"

Lady Damage said. "I seriously doubt the judge will reduce his sentence further."

"We can invite him back to the team after he is released," The Mystery said. "If he still wants to be a superhero."

"He didn't sound like he wanted to come back," Electric Boy said. "It's a shame. This is *his* team after all."

"I was surprised that Doctor Galaxy turned himself in," Lady Damage said. "Turns out, supervillains *can* change in prison. All they need is a real reason to change for the better, and Koolara showed it to Doctor Galaxy."

"Maybe Koolara should be a supervillain counsellor," Electric Boy mused.

"How was the visit to the hospital with Doctor Galaxy last evening?" Pandora Girl looked at me.

She was referring to Doctor Galaxy's visit to the hospital yesterday, where Samantha Stewart was nursing her health. He had been granted this one request on account of him helping to take down The Shock. He had requested for Koolara to come along, and I had agreed.

There had been at least ten policemen with us, watching for any sign of green smoke from Doctor Galaxy. They also carried a portable version of the Paralysis Serum detectors so that Doctor

Galaxy couldn't leave the parameters constructed by the ten policemen around him, but I knew that there was nothing to worry about.

Samantha Stewart was beautiful, and I could tell that she was a nice person. My heart ached when I saw her entire leg wrapped up in a fracture brace that looked like the most uncomfortable thing to wear. She would be able to return home soon, but it would be a long while before she could walk normally again.

"What I did was wrong," Doctor Galaxy had told her. "I shouldn't have tried to take revenge on the Super Secret. I should have been *here*, for you. I'm sorry."

"You're here now," she smiled. "And you did a good thing yesterday, Peter."

Peter held her hand in his and grinned. I knew that he was trying to save this moment.

"I saw your apology on TV," Samantha said, addressing me. "I don't blame the Super Secret for my injury. Please continue to be superheroes."

"It went well," I replied Pandora Girl, leaning back in my armchair. "Doctor Galaxy will be okay."

"What's going to happen to the Super Diamond?" Electric

Boy asked, turning to The Mystery. "It is safe to leave it with the police?"

"Yes, it is safe," The Mystery replied. "I already handed it to them this morning. It will be kept in the evidence storage facility with all the other supervillain crime evidence. I trust our police department."

"Did you discover anything new in the past three days?" Lady Damage asked.

"When the Super Diamond makes contact with your skin, an unknown chemical in the diamond connects with the part of your brain that controls your nature and personality. It heightens those components to an extreme level, leading your physical body to adapt and transform along with it. Thus, you can be incredibly strong or fast if the diamond causes your brain to amplify those attributes. That is how the diamond gives a human what we know as superpowers."

"So, the superpowers are actually like..." Lady Damage twirled a lock of her hair. "An enhancement of your character?"

"Yes," The Mystery actually sounded a little impressed. "The SuperNova wanted more strength such that he created the Nova Gloves, so the diamond gave him super strength. The Triple Dangers valued speed, so the diamond gave them super speed. The Shock prioritised protection, so the diamond made his entire body invincible. There is certainly a pattern here."

"So, I'll become super attractive?" Electric Boy said.

"Super annoying," Lady Damage coughed.

"Super brave," Pandora Girl giggled.

Lady Damage teased the new couple, and we all laughed, except The Mystery, of course. My eyes wandered to the seat next to me where The Shock usually sat, but now there was a glossy magazine on it. I picked it up and realised that it was the very first issue of Super Addict Magazine, published just days after our six-member team was formed.

The text on the cover, made to look like a comic book panel, was pretty catchy...

Diamond City is famous for three things. The sale of chewing gum is banned, each citizen's first and last name starts with the same letter, and most importantly, we have the Super Secret.

ACKNOWLEDGMENTS

A big THANK YOU to…

My family, friends and fans, for supporting this book.

Hillary Goh, for editing and improving my story.

Soefara, for the amazing character designs and book cover.

Samara Sketch, Flavia Bertoni and Stella Yap, for the beautiful illustrations.

And Tasha Arora, for the kind review.

THE SUPER SECRET
WILL RETURN

www.thesupersecretbook.com

@thesupersecretbook

#thesupersecretbook

Made in the USA
Middletown, DE
18 May 2020